A KING IMPERILED

A Historical Novel of Scotland

J. R. TOMLIN

Albannach Publishing

❀ Created with Vellum

INTRODUCTION

To help with clarifying how people are referenced, in medieval Scotland women did not take their husband's surname, so the wife of King James I and mother of King James II was always Joan de Beaufort. Noblemen were normally referred to by their title, so that the Earl of Douglas would be called Douglas. In many references works, you may find Alexander Livingston, Lord Callendar referred to as Livingston, but Lord Callendar is the more correct name. It is what I use.

In regard to the sister of King James who was deaf, she did indeed sign, the royal family reputedly having brought a tutor from Italy to teach her.

HISTORICAL CHARACTERS

IN APPROXIMATE ORDER OF APPEARANCE

- Sir Patrick Gray of Kinneff, Gentleman of the King's Bedchamber, Master of the Guard of King James II
- James Douglas of Avondale, later 7th Earl of Douglas, known as James the Gross
- Sir Andrew Gray, 1st Lord Gray, father of Sir Patrick Gray
- James Kennedy, Canon and later Bishop of Dunkeld and Saint Andrews
- Queen Joan de Beaufort, widow of murdered King James I, King of Scots mother of King James II
- Annabella Forbes, lady-in-waiting to Queen Joan de Beaufort, daughter of Alexander Forbes, 1st Lord Forbes
- James II, King of the Scots
- Archibald Douglas, 5th Earl of Douglas, titular Duke of Touraine, head of the Black Douglas Clan, Lieutenant General of Scotland
- William Crichton, Lord Crichton, Keeper of

Edinburgh Castle and for a time Chancellor of Scotland

- Alexander Livingston, Lord Callendar, Keeper of Stirling Castle, Justiciar of Scotland
- Earl William Douglas, 6th Earl of Douglas murdered at the 'Black Dinner', son of Archibald Douglas, 5th Earl of Douglas.
- David Douglas, younger brother of the 6th Earl of Douglas also slain at the Black Dinner
- Earl James Douglas, 3rd Earl of Angus, head of the Red Douglas clan
- Margaret, Dauphine of France, eldest sister of King James II (only by mention)
- Isabella, Duchess of Brittany, sister of King James II
- Eleanor, Archduchess of Austria, sister of King James II
- Mary, Countess of Buchan, sister of King James II
- Joan, *Muta Domina* of Dalkeith, Countess of Morton, sister of King James II, third daughter of Queen Joan and King James I
- Annabella, Countess of Huntley, youngest sister of King James II
- James Stewart, Black Knight of Lorne, second husband of Queen Joan
- Alexander Seton, Lord Gordon, 1st Earl of Huntly
- William Douglas, 8th Earl of Douglas, son of James the Gross
- Alexander Lindsay, 4th Earl of Crawford
- John Douglas, brother of the 8th Earl of Douglas, created Earl of Avondale
- John of Islay, Earl of Ross, son of Alexander of that ilk

- Alexander Forbes, 1st Lord Forbes, married to Mary Douglas, daughter of the Earl of Angus, and father of Annabella of that ilk.

I

MARCH 25, 1437

James Douglas, Earl of Avondale. He lumbered out the door of David's Tower, the royal residence within Edinburgh Castle. In spite of the chilling drizzle, Avondale was wearing no cloak. Sweat dribbled down his round cheeks into the folds of his double chins. He paused, smoothing his black velvet doublet over his belly, blocking the way like a ponderous mountain.

"Where are you going?" Avondale asked.

Patrick Gray pressed his lips together to hold back a sharp retort. "My father summoned me to meet with him here."

"He must have meant you to wait for him at Holyrood Kirk. We have important matters afoot here, preparing for the coronation. It's no place for a whelp."

It was none of the Earl of Avondale's business where his father summoned him, Patrick thought, but he was not going to dispute with him. James Douglas of Avondale was eaten with envy for the power his cousin the Black Douglas had. Everyone said so. Avondale was a rich holding, but not even a tiny fraction of the holdings and power of his cousin. He also resented that until the king was murdered, the Black Douglas had the king's ear. He no doubt resented the fact that his cousin would soon be lieutenant general of Scotland, but Patrick saw no reason the man should take out that ire on himself.

Bland faced, Patrick gave a polite nod. It was best to avoid arguments with any of the Douglases, even this one. "Mayhap, My Lord, but he said he awaited me here. I'd best find him."

"Do so then," Avondale said, passing into the watery morning light.

Patrick hurried through a long enfilade of stuffy rooms and waves of the scent of moth-herbs, wet wool, and oak smoke from hearth fires. Men huddled in corners whispering. Rumors must have run like wild fire since the king's murder. Had the gossips learned that the leader of the assassins, Robert Stewart, had implicated his grandfather, the Earl of Atholl, when he was captured?

Glances at him were wary. No one went anywhere for the nonce without a hand on their sword. Some nodded to Patrick as he passed but no one spoke.

When Patrick closed the door behind him, the inmost chamber was silent. His father, face haggard, stared into a small fire on the hearth. Without looking up he said, "Patrick. I expected you sooner."

Patrick sighed under his breath. He had been traveling since before daybreak from his father's home at Longforgan and in the saddle for most of the past three weeks, riding with the Earl of Angus as they hunted down the men who has assassinated King James. He had stopped at an inn only long enough to change out of his clothes that had been rain soaked and mud and dirt splattered to the shoulder. He hadn't even eaten since the night before.

James Kennedy, Canon of Dunkeld, youngish, thin, and

tonsured sat at a table scattered with documents, a flagon of wine, and a lit stand of candles. He gave Patrick a bleak smile.

Chilled from the drizzle, Patrick approached hearth and held out his hands. "I saw Avondale on my way. He said you're preparing for the coronation...here? Not in Scone?"

Kennedy motioned to the flagon of wine on the table. "You look fit to fall over from exhaustion, Sir Patrick. Sit and drink whilst we talk."

Patrick's father grunted, but with unusual patience for him, folded his hands behind his back and waited as Patrick poured a cup of wine and took a seat opposite Kennedy.

Kennedy folded his hands atop the pile of documents. "It is unheard of to have the coronation in Edinburgh. But the Earl of Atholl is still on the loose, and Scone is too near his lands. We will take nae chances with the life of our new king."

Patrick had just taken a drink of the wine, so it took a moment for him to swallow and ask, "You cannot think they would make an attempt on the prince's life."

"It was in their plans and was a near thing."

This was news to Patrick, but he'd been chasing down a murderer too far from Scone to hear such news. He'd not considered that they'd murder a child. "Aye, I suppose they would have to kill him as well."

Patrick's father shrugged, propped an elbow on the mantel, and considered his son like a merchant regarding his wares. At fifty, he was still as lean and fit as he must have been at thirty. He was dressed in his finest doublet of green satin and blue silk. His height and broad shoulders were still impressive, and his thick, gray hair gave him gravitas. "So tell me about catching up with Robert Stewart. How went the business?"

Evidently his questions were to be ignored. "As filthy as you'd expect and knee deep in snow for much of the chase. He was abandoned by most of his followers before we caught them. We only gave him a beating, since the queen wanted him alive."

"Go on," Kennedy said. As he listened to Patrick recount their long, hard ride through the Highlands led by the Earl of Angus, the churchman's face creased occasionally into an attentive frown. When Patrick described riding down Robert Stewart's party, he leaned forward and tilted his head. He poured a cup of wine and took a sip. After Patrick finished, he said, "After the coronation, Robert will nae last long. Tomorrow he shall be hanged, drawn and quartered. As will his grandsire when we lay hands on him."

"Not beheaded?" Patrick blurted. Scots had never copied this English method of execution.

"No," said Lord Gray. "Not beheaded. The trial will be only a formality, and it's already agreed upon."

At the behest of the English queen? Patrick decided to let the topic go. "So they meant to kill young James?" Patrick asked again. "And to make Atholl king?"

Kennedy shook his head in negation. "Not to make Atholl king, no, but if the lad were dead and one of his sisters married to Robert Stewart, that would have had the same affect. They would have ruled in her name."

Patrick's father cleared his throat. "That will nae happen, and our new liege lord shall be kept safe. That's why I sent for you."

"Why you sent for me? How so?"

"This afternoon wee James will be crowned. He will have a household of his own, gentlemen of the bedchamber, a master of his guard. And the master of the guard will be you."

"Wait." Patrick held up both hands and reared back. Since when did his father and Kennedy have the managing of the prince?

"What about the Earl of Douglas. Doesn't he have a say in this? What about the Queen?"

"We must have people we trust near James. Especially after..." Kennedy raised a thin eyebrow. "You may not have heard that James's tutor was part of the conspiracy. It was a near thing that the queen reached them before the news of the king's death did. The tutor awaited the news that the king was murdered to kill the lad. He tried to flee and died on the spot."

It is nearing mid-day. The wind had picked up and rattled the windows. The fire popped and blazed up, illuminating Kennedy's intense face. Patrick looked from Kennedy to his father.

"I take it I have no say in the matter of my position."

Kennedy flicked the question away with a slight motion of his hand. "We must quickly gather matters in hand. With Atholl at large there is still a possibility of an uprising and always a danger of an English invasion. But discounting the assassins, who with the grace of God will be dead soon enough, nobles the late king had trampled will be panting for power. Some such as Erskine will do anything possible to gain lands and titles that have been seized by the crown. We cannot give them time to gather forces. God wot, Bishop Cameron being out of the country with the Pope in Bologna is no help. No one kens which way the power of the Black Douglas will swing. The king had the Douglas well under his thumb but now..." A shake of his head was accompanied by a thoughtful frown. "There is nae way to ken what Douglas will do. We must act with surety and steadiness. Our first act must be putting our people into the king's household."

"Will James nae continue to bide with the queen?"

"While he is so young a lad, his place is with his mother." Kennedy picked up a quill from beside the scattered documents. "We are preparing an act for parliament giving her control of his grace and funds for his keeping, but he must have his own household as befits a king. You will be part of it. And you shall see that he remains safe."

Did Kennedy have his eye on being chancellor, Patrick wondered. While the king had lived, no one would have replaced Bishop Cameron in the king's trust. But with a child king and Cameron in Bologna and out of favor with the Pope Eugene besides, who could know? Kennedy was only a canon and sub-deacon of Dunkeld, but that would not debar him. He was after all a cousin to the late king and to his son. He was the son of the late Lord Kennedy and brother of that present lord. He had studied somewhere in France, but if he was a scholar and learned was beyond Patrick's ken. Patrick decided he might as well ask. "What about the chancellor? Will it still be Cameron?"

His father shook his head. "With Cameron to be retained out of the kingdom for only the Pope knows how long, another must be named. When he returns, then we shall see."

"But whom will be named?"

"After the coronation, there will be a parliament to discuss that matter and others, but I expect it to be Lord Callendar." Kennedy was studying a document before him, half filled with writing. He looked up. "Sir Patrick, why such hesitation over a signal honor?"

Patrick could not refuse the task, but did they not understand what they were demanding it of him. "I think this is... beyond me, sir. The king murdered. Threats to our young prince. The kingdom teetering on the edge of chaos and you task me with keeping our liege safe? Why not someone... more experienced? I...I fear I would fail. I am nae skilled in political cunning. Why me?"

"Because you are told to," his father snapped out. "You know how to use that sword at your belt, do you not?"

"Aye, My Lord. You ken that I do."

"I expect you to use that to defend wee James should it

ever come to it. And you shall use the brain in your head to gather information. You are likable enough. You will gain the lad's trust, so he will want you close to him. That will allow you to learn everything that goes on in his household, what those around him say and think, and thus, so shall we."

Patrick rubbed the back of his neck as he tried to piece together what they wanted of him. "You want me to act as a spy. But it is the queen's household as well." He shook his head. "I dinnae understand."

Kennedy leaned forward, his still youthful face creased in a deep frown. "Sir Patrick, every powerful lord in Scotland will vie for control of our boy king. And I tell you, I am nae sure that we can keep them from gaining it. His mother, our good queen, will try to hold onto the regency, but she has only a small power base. What side will the Black Douglas take? Will Angus side with him? I am nae sure who they will support when it comes to a power play. Nor is William Crichton a man to be dismissed. He is of no great family, but he has powerful friends. If anything goes wrong, even the smallest of things, James could fall into the hands of enemies, as did his father for so many years. And nothing would ensue but danger and chaos."

"Crichton? Really?" Yes, Crichton held Edinburgh Castle for the king but the Crichton family had never been of any great importance.

"Enough," Lord Gray said. "You shall serve the lad, make yourself pleasant to all, make no enemies, and give no one reason to separate you from him. Keep him safe at all costs."

"And spy for you."

Kennedy nodded. "So you may call it if you like."

2

The bailey yard of Edinburgh Castle was filled with a jostling crowd. They milled about in their velvet and silk finery, gems gleaming, as the sun broke through the clouds. It took a huge number of people to fill the castle bailey, by far the largest Patrick had ever seen. It was more than two hundred yards across from the gate to the east wall, surrounded by walls higher than three men.

The Royal Chapel stood in one far corner, cut off from the bailey by its own low wall. There was a large vegetable garden beside the chapel. David's Tower loomed one hundred feet high, a grim building of gray stone so missive it cut off half the sky. The great hall, not nearly as tall but longer, stood across from the main gate, chimneys poking up, with high, narrow windows, the ones flanking the wide door giving the front a look like a face gaping out at them. There was a huge stable where horses were being led out, a dungeon, housing for the garrison, a practice yard with dummies set up, and a workshop for manufacturing weapons.

At least the naked stone on which the castle stood meant his shoes and chausses were not instantly mud splashed as he shouldered through the crowd. A little distance away, Patrick's cousin Padraig Maclellan waved frantically. He was middling height, with a sharp face. He had tempted Patrick into more than a little mischief when they were lads. Patrick grinned and waved back.

He was half way to reaching Padraig when he saw his father, standing with the queen, motioned to him. He grimaced at Padraig and headed that way instead.

Queen Joan de Beaufort, in her mid-thirties, was full-figured from much childbearing but tall and regal with striking blue eyes and a firm chin. Dressed in silken mourning white that shimmered in the sunlight, she was breathtaking. When he got nearer he saw that yellow remains of a bruise marred half her face. Across her forehead, a half-healed cut disfigured her forehead. Blemished as her face was by the attack, Patrick could still see why as a maiden she had been the object of the king's love poems.

When he finally wormed his way through the crowd to the queen's party, Patrick bowed low.

She offered her hand to be kissed. "Ah, Sir Patrick, your father and Canon Kennedy have spoken highly of you."

"I'm eager to be at your service in any way that I may, Your Grace."

She turned to look at her children where they were gathered. James, in a fine purple cloak and bonnet, had the large eyes and long nose of the Stewarts, but a livid red birthmark splashed across his left cheek. Two of his six sisters, both with shimmering blond hair like their mother, stood with him. Another sister was in France and married to France's Dauphin. The others, too young for a long ceremony, were evidently to be left behind. It was an oddly hushed group for healthy children, all wide-eyed and looking nervously about.

"James, come to me," the queen called.

Turning back to Patrick she continued, "It is for my son's

service I would have you. I must have someone with him I can trust to keep him safe." She pressed her fingers to her forehead and tightly closed her eyes. After a moment, she regained her poise and went on. "Trust comes hard after being murderously betrayed by men so close to us."

The six-year-old prince, a tall lad, reedy as though growing fast, reached her side and she took his hand. He had his father's chestnut hair and wide, piercing blue eyes. Patrick thought he would probably grow into a fine looking man in spite of the red birthmark. Fiery Face he had heard the lad called.

"James, this is Sir Patrick. He is now the master of your guard and will protect you. With his life, if need be."

James gave him a long, searching look. "They murdered my father. So..." He blinked two or three times. "You must not let them murder me."

"He is young for such an important position," said a tall man Patrick did not recognize with a short, dark beard, finely dressed in red silk lined and sleeves edged in marten. He looked closely at Patrick with dark eyes and then cast a pointed look at James who stared at the both of them wide-eyed.

The queen shook her head. "Would you take on the job, Sir James? I'd trust the Black Knight of Lorne as I would few others, but I think you have other duties."

It was Sir James Stewart then, someone he'd had no cause to meet previously. Patrick nodded in acknowledgement. "I am young, Sir James, but my sword and my life are the king's." He would have knelt to his new liege lord, child though he was, but instead squatted so as not to soil the knees of his best chauses. "I swear to you, Your Grace, no harm shall come to you. Not as long as I draw breath."

"Your Grace," a voice boomed behind him, and Patrick rose. Approaching was a burly, broad-shouldered man, black hair and beard liberally streaked with gray, Archibald Douglas, Fifth Earl of Douglas. He was trailed by two youths, from the resemblance obviously his sons. The older, in his early teens, swaggered a bit but the younger brother looked about with wide-eyed curiosity.

The earl bowed deeply and kissed the queen's hand.

"How well-grown your lads are since I last saw them," she said. "Mayhap they might keep James company on the way to Holyrood Abbey."

The two older lads looked uncertainly at the young king who instantly forgot he was doubtless supposed to be on his dignity.

"I'm riding to the Abbey," he told them. "Are you?" They nodded and he asked where their horses were. At nods from the adults, the three scurried towards horses still being led from the stable. "This is my first real horse," James chattered as they went. "Not a pony and mine own!"

"A few moments distraction may help him to endure the long ceremony," the queen murmured when the three were out of hearing. She watched with a smile as her son preened, showing his new friends the finer points of his horse. Around them dozens of mounts were being readied.

"Aye and parliament he must attend after the coronation," the earl said. "With serious decisions to be made. That may be a long affair, so mayhap we should nae delay."

Queen Joan looked around at the packed bailey. "You are right, of course, My Lord. It is time."

On her signal, heralds shouted to make ready. Riders shouted for their mounts, horses snorted, and harness clanked above the clatter of hooves. The Earl of Argyll, a big fair-haired man in with a wind chapped face, clad in cherry velvet and yellow silk, helped the royal children to mount. Douglas knelt and held his hands in a stirrup to lift the queen onto her horse. Patrick swung into the saddle and nudged his horse to a few horse's lengths behind the young king.

Horns blew and the heralds shouted to let the royal party through. Drummers and trumpeters started up at the front. The excitement had all the horses stamping and snorting, but shortly the queen with the prince beside her formed the head of the procession. All around them, jostling nobles argued about the order of precedence as heralds urged them into a column.

At last, they rode through the portcullis gate and between the hulking bastions that guarded the way over the draw bridge. Patrick stayed as close to James as courtesy allowed, but the two Douglas lads rode beside him, the older bragging that his father would soon allow him to tilt in the list. He had much to say about his skill with the lance.

Soon any speech was drowned by noise. Cheering crowds lined the way along the Via Regis and through the city to Holyrood Abbey. The thronged streets rang with shouts of, "God bless the King! Wee Jamie Stewart! God save the King's Grace!' The soon-to-be king grinned and waved hard to the onlookers.

At the end of the Via Regis, within high stone walls of the monastery, the twin towers of Holyrood Abbey rose as grand as a cathedral, centuries old and breathtaking in its magnificence. All around spread extensive monastic buildings, gardens sparkling with the light green of early spring, and a palatial marble abbot's residence.

The trumpeters were blowing another fanfare as the king reached the abbey steps. The way was already thronged when they dismounted. The sounds of choir and instruments and hundreds of voices from rolled through the doors like a tide as they entered the abbot's door into the vestry where the press of bodies and waves of conflicting smells of incense, musk, burning candles and wet fur nearly choked him.

Patrick barely had time to pick out familiar faces, men he'd seen in his father's company, the Earl of Argyll; Alexander Nairne, Lord Lyon King of Arms; Robert de Keith, the Marischal of Scotland; Bishop Ochiltree who would conduct the ceremony and more he couldn't even put a name to. The queen, soon to be queen mother, the princesses, and all of their ladies bustled out through a side passage to the choir stalls where they would not suffer the press of the hundreds within the abbey. He moved with the throng into the abbey itself.

Columns soared to impossible heights, casting long shadows across the crowd. Courtiers filled most of the front, although in the rear crowded some of the rabble. Patrick had no desire to put himself forward in this exalted company, although he felt he must stay within sight of the king, who had begun biting his lower lip and looking about nervously. Why wouldn't he? It had to be impossible to know whom to trust when members of your own family had murdered your father.

Patrick managed to give him a reassuring smile. He had to wonder if the lad would ever again completely trust that those around him didn't mean murder. How many might? The crowd made Patrick twitch with nerves. Anything could happen with so many around the king, but surely he was safe with the Douglas and the Earl of Argyll so near. He shook off the thought.

The voices of the choir rose in a final soaring: *Propter domum Domini Dei nostri, quæsivi bona tibi.*

Trumpets blared. Patrick found his gaze roving. Gilt candle stands alight with beeswax tapers cast nimbuses over the garlands and runners. But it was still shadowy in the corners and behind the painted columns.

With ceremonial flourish, Alexander Nairne, the Lord Lyon, led the king to the throne-like chair placed in front of the altar. Fortunately someone had thought to place a step stool next to it so the lad could clamber up into the great seat. When the Bishop Ochiltree, a man of middling size and years and a great friend of the dead king, approached and began a long Latin prayer, the lad watched him tensely.

At last the prayer was done. Standing next to the throne, Nairne took out a long scroll and proclaimed the lineage of the Kings of the Scots, beginning with King Vipoig, through the Pictish kings, on to King Gartnait, and on and on to the great King Cináed mac Ailpín through King Máel Coluim, and finally to King Robert the First, King David the Second, King Robert the Second and King James the First.

Bishop Ochiltree lifted high a gold embossed ampulla, intoned a prayer of thanksgiving, and carried the container of sacred oil to the king. Once more the massed voices of the choir rose as the bishop anointed the king on each of his hands, above his heart and on the forehead.

William de le Haye carried the Sword of State, an enormous bejeweled weapon, to lay it across James's lap. When it slipped sideways, de le Haye quickly lifted it and stood to the side to hold it before him point down, as ceremonial guard. The Earl of Argyll knelt to press the Scepter of Scotland into James's hands. The boy fumbled the heavy thing and there was a gasp, but he managed to grasp it before it tumbled. He grinned with satisfaction and held it up proudly to the onlookers.

The Earl of Douglas entered, carrying the crown. Patrick breathed out a soft snort. The Douglases were truly in power if they were now crowning the king, but on second thought he realized that there was no one else to do so. It should have been the duty of the Earl of Atholl who was being pursued for plotting regicide.

In fact, the earl only touched the crown to the king's forehead because it was far too large to fit on his small head.

"God save the king!" Douglas shouted as he raised the crown high and the youngster beamed up at him.

The crowd took up the cry. "God save the King!" resounded off the high marble walls in a deafening cacophony. Patrick joined the shout as his ears rang with the noise. Church bells tolled and clanged, first above their heads in the high towers of the abbey and soon echoed from across the city.

Bishop Ochiltree knelt, took the young king's hands between his own and swore an oath of fealty. He rose, and the Earl of Argyll took his place. In a booming voice, the earl declared his loyalty.

Douglas, still holding the crown, looked a bit frantic as he tried to find somewhere suitable to place the crown while he took his own oath. The bishop reached for it and Douglas reluctantly gave it into his hands. He knelt and took his oath. A line was forming as the great ones scrambled into place to swear their fealty. Lord Lyon hustled his heralds out to check a few who put themselves out of their place. Voices were raised as they disputed precedence, but a scowl from the Lyon quieted argument.

With a flex of his shoulders, Patrick straightened and walked to take his place in the long line. They shuffled along, air musty with the scent of incense and sweat. Patrick stared at the velvet clad back of the man who preceded him, wondering how long it would take for them to reach the king. At last, the man knelt, mumbled the words and it was Patrick's turn.

He looked into the face of the boy who was now their king and returned the lad's faint smile. Dropping to his knees, he took James's hands, a child's hand to wield a royal scepter. *Jesu save us.*

"I, Patrick Gray, become your man in life and in death, faithful and loyal to you against all men that live, move or die.

I declare you to be my liege lord and none other—so may God help me and all the Saints."

For a moment, the boy king's hands tightened on his, and he felt within bones as fine as a bird's wing. "By the favor of God, I take you as my man to defend and to aid in all that I do."

With a sigh, Patrick rose and went to wait at the side, thankful each oath was short. He was sworn in life and death to this boy, and he'd try not to think about where his true loyalty might lie. He'd pray to the saints he never had it tested.

The fealty-taking still dragged on. And on. By the time the end of the line reached the throne, King James sagged in his throne, shoulders drooping from fatigue. Or perhaps from boredom, because he instantly sprang erect when the Earl of Douglas, shouted, "God save the King. Long live King James!"

The once more assembly took up the shout.

As the gathered guests continued shouting "God Save the King," James hopped down from the high throne. He looked up at Douglas who thrust his chin toward the Abbey's nave. James grinned in obvious relief and scampered through the nave toward the door where the royal ladies gathered. Douglas and Angus followed. The crowd parted to let them pass. Patrick shoved through the press, stepping on toes and elbowed anyone who didn't move.

Trumpets blared.

Outside was pandemonium. The sun was shining, and a cool March wind scattered rags of clouds across the sky. Douglas hoisted the king onto his horse. The horses stamped and shook their manes. Crichton, a short, hard-bitten man with a tanned face, was helping the queen, her daughters and ladies to mount. The red-haired, burly Earl of Angus hurried over to boost one of the princesses onto her mount. Heralds begged people to form up according to precedence. Patrick was as weary of ceremony as the soon-to-be king who was bouncing in the saddle with impatience to be off. The queen sidled her horse closer to him and said something in his ear.

Lord Gray lifted an eyebrow at Patrick and scowled. Perhaps he was judged not near enough to the king, but the street was a madhouse as the nobles impatiently urged their horses forward once more to the blaring of trumpets and bagpipes and the rumble of drums. An argument broke out between two sweating, velvet clad noblemen. Several put their heels to their mounts and trotted ahead, ignoring shouts from the heralds. The queen shrugged and nudged her horse to a walk. Glowering, the Black Douglas shouted for all to follow the king. The heralds gave up on keeping hereditary order, and the irregular procession, now closer to a mob, set up back toward Edinburgh Castle, bathed in afternoon sunlight.

Patrick's stomach grumbled and he sighed. Next would be long hours of the parliament and no hope of a meal any time in the near future.

3

The great hall of Edinburgh castle, an oblong chamber that reached from one side of the keep to the other, still had the polished look of being newly and richly refurbished. The high oak ceilings and the paneling, bosses intricately carved with foliage and corners of silver-gilt moldings, sparkled and gleamed. Torches flickered in silver sconces high on marble columns. Before the high carved fireplace was a dais with a gilded chair and a ponderous table stacked with parchments held down by a massive gavel.

A steady stream of noblemen filed through the doors as Patrick protested that he was not needed at the parliament. He could only imagine how tedious the old men's debate would be.

His father speared him with a dour look. "I expect your presence in the gallery. The queen will be there as well as several of her ladies. Make yourself pleasant, but attend all that is said on the floor as well as in the gallery."

Patrick rubbed his hollow stomach but it seemed to have given up on ever receiving food. It no longer even grumbled.

He gave his father a grudging bow and trudged up the narrow steps to the gallery that would normally be given over the musicians. Queen Joan stood at the railing and three ladies-in-waiting with her.

She smiled at him. "You are kind, Sir Patrick, to lend us your company. Looking on while they talk and talk and taking no part becomes..." She gave a wry shrug. "...tedious."

Below there was murmuring, shuffling and scraping of benches as hundreds of nobles took their places, earls, lords, bishops, mitered abbots and even a few wealthy merchants representing the royal burghs. 'I am happy to keep you company." He kissed her hand. "Hopefully, I can break the tedium somewhat."

"I am right sorry to put my poor ladies through the dreary affair, but it must be." Her tone did not sound all that sorry, and she had good reason for sharp interest in the proceedings. She motioned to the young woman with her who smiled at him. "Lady Annabella Forbes." The girl was splendid in green silk and a gauzy veil. She was perhaps sixteen, brown haired and brown eyed, slender and lovely, her creamy skin marred only by a sprinkling of freckles across her nose.

Queen Joan took the hand of a lady-in-waiting in her late twenties, tall and dignified blond hair beneath a modest wimple. "Lady Barbara Campbell who stood beside me so bravely on that dire day." Lady Barbara nodded to him but turned back to watch the confusion below. She nodded to an older woman, "And wife to Sir Alexander Callendar, Lady Janet Dundas." Lady Janet gave him a brief nod.

Lady Annabella made her courtesy to him with a solemn look. "You will be one of the king's gentlemen of the bedchamber, sir?"

"Yes, my lady—" He broke off at a flourish of trumpets. As he turned to watch, King James was ushered in by the Lord Lyon. The lad clambered up the stool and squirmed onto the huge throne. The Earl Marischal and the High Constable took their places behind the throne. The young king gazed around, wide eyed, but he settled back, his legs sticking straight out on the enormous gilded seat. He crossed his arms and seemed to have settled in to watch the show.

The Earl of Douglas marched up to a table placed near the throne and bowed. "With Your Grace's permission, I declare the parliament in session."

Well coached, James piped up with a loud, "Aye, My Lord Earl, you have my permission."

Douglas called for Bishop Ochiltree to begin the proceedings with a prayer for aid from the Almighty in dealing with the kingdom's grave loss, which prayer was mercifully short to Patrick's relief. The queen sat in a large chair placed there for her and Patrick snagged a seat next to Lady Annabella on a padded bench. He suspected she would be more congenial company than the other women.

When he looked back down, Douglas had turned to the onlookers and stated in a voice intended to carry across battlefields, "As you ken, the late king's chancellor, Bishop Cameron, was called to Bologna by the Pope Eugene and may be detained there for some time. But the kingdom's urgent business cannot wait for his return. As the most senior earl in the kingdom—" A buzz interrupted him. Of course the Earl of Atholl was more senior, but he was not here and when the queen laid hands on him he would not live long. Douglas slammed his palm down on the table with a resounding bang. "As the most senior earl in the kingdom not under attainder for treason, I call for the election of a new chancellor."

There were cries of agreement, so Douglas continued, "We must have a chancellor in the kingdom to keep order. Otherwise we are too tempting a target for an invasion. Or God forfend, there could even be an uprising. Therefore, we need a chancellor with experience in leading armed men.

Bishop Cameron has done great service to the realm, but it is time for skills that are not those of a churchman."

To Patrick's surprise, his father stood to speak. "The keeper of one of the royal castles, known to be trusted by our dead king, would be best for the position. I suggest we name Sir Alexander Callendar, Lord of Callendar. As the keeper of Stirling Castle, few men stood higher in the late king's trust."

There was a general murmur of agreement, but the Earl of Angus, head of the Red Douglas clan, jumped to his feet. "The king trusted many men, some to his grief. Another high in his council was Sir William Crichton, Lord Crichton, keeper of Edinburgh Castle. Edinburgh Castle is essential to defense of the realm. I believe he is best placed to defend the realm should such be needed and trusted as much as Callendar ever was. As Master of the Royal Household no one was higher in the esteem of our late king or better placed now to defend our kingdom."

When the queen gave a faint murmur, Patrick glanced sidelong at her. She looked down frowning for a moment, but smoothed her expression as she raised her gaze. Patrick realized that the Earl of Douglas was looking up at her, his heavy features stolid but an eyebrow raised.

Patrick's father had turned to stare at Angus, his lips squashed into a thin line. Obviously, this was a surprise and not a pleasant one. Did this mean that the power of the Douglases would be thrown behind Crichton? The Earl of Angus, from the branch of the family known as the Red Douglases, did not speak for the Black Douglas. In fact, they were usually at odds.

Canon Kennedy rose, "Sirs, I believe that Sir Alexander —" But he was cut off by a dozen voices arguing. The Thane of Glamis jumped to his feet and shouted something that was lost in the noise. The Lord of Dalkieth, another Douglas, was shouting at his cousin as well.

The Earl of Douglas grabbed up the gavel and pounded on the table. "Silence!" he bellowed. "Silence!" He paused until the tumult had died down and said, "I second the nomination of Sir William Crichton. Does anyone second that of Lord Callendar?"

Someone cursed. Patrick craned his neck but couldn't decide who it had been. No one spoke. For a long moment the hall seemed frozen, but the Earl of Angus slowly rose, his face twisted into an angry scowl. "I do."

The Earl nodded and asked if anyone else had a nomination.

Patrick snorted softly through his nose, and the queen glanced his way. She gave a tiny shake of her head. As he expected, no one cared to put forward another nomination in opposition to the Douglas faction.

The earl called for those supporting Crichton to raise their hands. Almost every hand in the hall went up. Lady Janet sucked in a noisy breath; the queen gave her arm a brief pat. Lady Annabella was biting her lip. Patrick wondered what she thought of the turn of events.

On the floor of the chamber, Crichton was striding briskly to the table on the dais. He bowed to the king and took up the chancellor's gavel. He hammered it a few times although the hall was already in silence as men glanced at each other. There would be many whispered conversations once the hall cleared, Patrick was sure. Already power alliances were shifting.

Crichton cleared his throat. "Nothing is more important than preventing an invasion from the south, so the first order of business is to declare the Earl of Douglas as Lieutenant General of Scotland. Is there any objection?"

This had been a foregone conclusion and in effect Douglas had already been functioning as lieutenant general since the king's murder. The declaration was met with profound silence.

Douglas bowed first to the throne and then to the assembly. "I am already gathering my forces in the border lands." The Earl of Angus rose to say he would join his forces to maintain the peace.

Patrick studied the men below. He could not see their faces, but shoulders were gradually relaxing and backs losing their stiffness. The position of the Black Douglas was clear and that simplified everyone's course, for few would care to dispute him. Patrick almost smiled as he thought probably none would, not even Kennedy or his father. But neither man looked pleased.

An hour of discussion of whose forces would take up which position and who would invade the lands of the Earl of Atholl to bring him to Edinburgh for trial had Patrick stifling yawns behind his hand. This was followed by arguments over appointments to some minor offices and the raising of revenues. When his stomach grumbled loudly, Annabella giggled softly.

At last Patrick's father stood. "My lords, we have not yet decided on a Council of Regency. This is a matter of such import that it cannot be delayed. Money must be allotted for the queen. The king's household must be discussed."

"Aye," Crichton said. "But that is not a matter for the full parliament."

Patrick's father was scowling when Crichton named a committee to choose the Council of Regency that did not include him. He made no response when Kennedy was named to it, but a glance passed between the two men.

Suddenly, one of the doors banged open, and a man-at-arms rushed in, a guard protesting futilely behind him.

"He's captured! Word just came from Lothian." He was beaming. "Atholl was taken as he fled for England."

4

MARCH 26, 1427

Patrick knew it was a dream because he had dreamt it before.

In his dream his father was with him as he had been on that day. The walls of Longforgan manor were draped in mist that shifted and moved as he looked up the stairs. Torches high on the walls cast shadows that twisted and writhed. Margaret screamed, and his skin crawled with horror. How long had she been screaming?

He could stand it no longer. He had to go to her. When he started for the stairs, his father blocked his way.

"They're hurting her," Patrick shouted.

"It always hurts. You can only wait," his father answered.

When another shriek rent the air, Patrick dodged around his father. Hard fingers grasped his arm. "You would only make it worse. It's no place for a man."

When he stopped his struggle, his father patted his shoulder. "It has been a long time coming. Poor lass. But it will soon be over."

"Two days. She has been screaming for two days, and the bairn will not come."

When his father turned away, Patrick bolted. The stairs were so thick with the fog, he could not see the top. It wrapped around him to tight it was like running through deep water. She shouted, "Patrick!" He thrashed to get free of the binding wrapped around him.

"Patrick!"

"I'm coming," he whispered. "Margaret, I'm coming."

"Patrick," a man's voice said.

He half-woke and kicked free of the blankets tangled around his legs and stared at a stone wall, not Longforgan. The stone was darker and grim.

"Patrick, are you all right?" Boyd asked, half dressed in braes, chausses and a linen shirt.

Patrick gaped at him. "Huh?"

"You look like you just found the gates of hell in that wall."

Patrick looked at Boyd for a second, and then back at the wall. *God's bones*. He sat up and pulled himself together. "Aye, I just had a dream about..." He shrugged. "It does nae matter what it was about."

"The queen wants us to attend the king early."

"Does she?" Patrick muttered. It was a duty but a new one that he longed to throw off. The chamber was cold, and Patrick's head felt muzzy as though he'd not slept at all. Some nights like the last he did not sleep well, nights when his memories and his grief crept out of the locked room of his heart where he stored them. They had been too young when they'd married. She too young for having a child, he too young to know how to protect her. Such nights he might sleep but such sleep was not rest, and the following day his head ached. But he had given his young king an oath that no harm would come to him, so if the day filled him with dismay, he had his duty.

Boyd grabbed up a green doublet, shoved his arms into it

and said, chattering jauntily, "I am going to go down and find a bite of bread and some ale before I go to the queen's solar. Who knows when we'll have a chance later? You'd better hurry up, or I'll eat what there is."

After he was gone, Patrick arose and opened the shutters all the way. The sky above was clear and glittering for a day that would soon be so grim. He shuddered and turned from the window to pour water from the pitcher into a bowl, and splashed his face until some of the fog cleared.

He was only twenty-two but on mornings like this he felt a decade older. He'd have to become accustomed to being surrounded by the youths of the child king's household and the chattering princesses. They flitted around him with their untouched lives, full of hope and confidence. Patrick wanted to shake them and tell them to stop being so happy; it would go to the devil in no time. And then he remembered that the queen's life had done exactly that. Self-pity was a venal and ugly thing, he thought.

The water was tepid. Servants must have brought warm it at Prime, but it had long since cooled. He felt his cheeks. He had to shave as well, so he grabbed up the soap and lathered his face, shaved, and ran the cloth over his arms and legs.

When he had toweled off, he opened his small kist. Eventually clothing from home would reach him, but for the time he had little to choose from. He had to wonder what garment was appropriate for an execution. He supposed whatever he had would have to do, so he donned a shirt, dark chausses, and his second best doublet, the one of heavy blue wool brightened with yellow ribbons.

He gazed out over the vista that was beyond his new home. Arthur's Seat towered high above Edinburgh town and even higher, a hundred feet in the air towered David's Tower, casting a long shadow in the morning light. Below he could see the inner bailey and the stable where horses were led out looking like toys. Beyond were the hills bathed in splashes of purple and yellow and green.

He considered going below for there would be bread and and ale for breaking the fast, but he was not sure he wanted food in his stomach for what was to come. Instead he ran down the winding stairs a single flight to the queen's solar. Patrick heard the murmur of voices even before he opened the door. Queen Joan sat as Lady Janet fastened the mesh of jeweler's work that formed the queen's headdress. Janet tutted slightly as she patted it into a stylized horn shape. Isabella, the next oldest of the king's sisters, a lass of twelve years, was reading aloud in French to her mother from some book.

Joanna, the little mute lady they called her, held a doll with one hand and made motions with her other to another princess. Was that Princess Mary? Yes, he was sure that was Mary who was so close to Joanna in age they might almost have been twins. Mary made a motion back as and the two seemed to understand each other perfectly as they put the doll into a toy crib and covered it. James was on his knees working the arm of a wooden knight up and down and crowing, "Have at you!" to an imaginary opponent. Lady Annabella stood at a large cabinet putting away some of the queen's clothing.

His father nodded to him, looking grim.

Patrick bowed low to the queen and for a moment wondered if he should also bow to the young king, but the lad paid him no mind.

"Ah, Sir Patrick, how are you settling in this drear place?" She offered her hand for him to kiss. "I hope you do not find your chamber too grim."

"I've been made most comfortable, my lady. You've been kindness itself, and my belongings will soon arrive from home."

“It has been sunny for the season,” Lady Janet said as she gave another pat to the queens glittering headdress. “I pray that it will last through the day.”

“Oh, leave off, Janet. My headdress is well enough. And I care naught for the sun.” Her jaw tightened and her voice grew harsh and low. “Let the sun, the sky, and all the world see Robert Stewart pay for his treachery. Foul murderer that he is.” She tightened her slender hands into fists and held them before her, a look of intense hatred washing over her features. “He was our cousin, our chamberlian. That we trusted the foul traitor...”

Patrick was left speechless and a hushed silence fell over the room as the children stared at their mother. Robert Stewart, who had done foul treachery at his grandsire's behest, would be executed shortly, leaving only the Earl who had planned it yet to die.

She took a deep breath and stood, forcing a smile that curved her mouth but did not reach her eyes. She waited until the children went back to their games before she continued. "And when we return, we pack to leave. My lord husband hated this grim pile, and we shall not abide here."

"Where will we go?" Patrick burst out. If his father or Kennedy knew of this plan, they had not mentioned it to him. He was sure they did not, and his father silently raised an eyebrow.

"First to Holyrood Abbey. We have pleasant chambers there. From there we'll go to Dunfirmline Palace for the nonce. With the miscreant Atholl no longer at large, it will be quite safe for my son. And it is certainly a more pleasing than...Edinburgh Castle." She spit the name as though it were poison. "My husband disliked this place. He always said that it is more prison than home. Once this duty is done, we shall depart."

Lord Gray opened his mouth, but then closed it looking

thoughtful. After a moment he said, "It will be a relief to all of us when the traitor is dead."

The queen stood and nodded sharply. "My ladies, gather the children. They have a right to see justice done." Head held stiffly high she turned for the door.

As Lady Annabella and Lady Janet herded the children after her, Patrick shot his father a questioning look, but received only a shake of the head in response. And then he followed the others out the door and down the stairs to join Sir James of Lorne and Lord Crichton.

All the way road up the slope of Calton Hill, the air was filled with shouts from the crowd lining the way. "God save our wee King! King Jamie!" It was a press of men and women, shouting, faces flushed with excitement. A group of boys chased screeching after them as they approached the gallows. Men-at-arms took their horses' reins as they dismounted. The roar of the crowd was deafening.

Patrick followed the queen and her children up the wooden steps of the pavilion. Above their heads the red awning rippled in the breeze. There was a chair for the king piled with a couple of pillows, so he could easily see over the low barrier in the front. Beside him the queen also took a chair. There were long benches on each side for the court.

Patrick watched as they dozen of their party took their places. There was room to sit, but he propped a shoulder against the back wall and crossed his arms, frowning. This thing of hanging, drawing and beheading was the way of execution of traitors in England, so he had heard tell. Everyone knew it was how Sir William Wallace had been so foully murdered by England's King Edward Longshanks. But it left a bad taste in his mouth. Scottish ways were not the same as English. Still... the queen had a right to her vengeance. No one could deny that.

The screams and shouts of the crowd reached a crescendo

as a mounted man-at-arms reached the top of the hill. Behind him, dragged by his bound hands stumbled Robert Stewart, naked, bloodied from head to foot from the torture used to extract his confession. On each side marched a line of men-at-arms to protect him from the enraged crowd. A rock sailed between them to thud at the miscreant's feet.

The black hooded executioner stood arms akimbo on the gallows. Next to him was a long table. A couple of men-at-arms grabbed Stewart by the arms and dragged him, feet dragging, up the steps. The executioner draped the hanging noose around the man's neck and motioned to the men-at-arms to hoist him up. He would be lowered before he could die. The hanging was humiliation, not death sentence.

Patrick winced when Stewart thudded, barely conscious and moaning, onto the wooden boards to be hoisted onto the waiting table. He glanced at the young king who had turned white and had pressed a hand to his mouth. Stewart shrieked under the executioner's knife. But the child king never took his eyes from the man who had murdered his father as again a shriek ripped the air.

Shortly it was all over.

When they returned, everyone was quiet. Lady Janet took the quiet, white-faced king to his chamber. The lad had never looked away as Stewart's intestines were cut out while he still lived and thrown into a fire. At the stench, Patrick had had to swallow down sour bile.

It should have been a clean beheading, not the tradition of torturous execution from England. But none could gainsay the queen. Only once he was tortured to death had his head been cleanly cut from his body.

The queen looked as though a huge weight had lifted from her. For the first time since yesterday's coronation, her forehead wasn't creased or her mouth drawn up in a tense line. The hall was quiet. A sole guard stood beside the doors while a servant boy knelt adding a faggot to the flames in the hearth. A manservant set a tray with a flagon of wine and goblets on table and poured. Crichton took one and handed another to the queen. Boyd took one as well but Patrick shook his head. Annabella, who still looked quite pale, just turned away.

Patrick's father looked out one of the high arched windows, his back to them.

The queen smiled into her goblet and said, "At last, that worry is done. My son is safe."

"Of course, Your Grace." Crichton's self-important tone grated on Patrick's raw nerves. "I shall see that he is always kept safe, but you ken that Stewart and Atholl were nae the only threat to the king."

She raised her chin. "Your duty is Edinburgh Castle and serving as chancellor. I have ample men-at-arms to see that my son is protected. They shall do so."

"You?" He twisted his mouth into a smile. "Your grace, no one expects you to guard the king. No one would expect it of a woman. That is why I have him here surrounded by my guards and in this strong fortress."

She crossed her arms tight across her breast. "You are mistaken, My Lord. For I am not a mere woman, but a queen. On the morn, we leave for Holyrood Abbey."

"I have the trust of the Lieutenant General of Scotland in this matter." His lips formed a tight smile. "He trusts me to protect the king. This I shall do. Here he shall stay. Under my care and protection."

The color drained from the queen's face and her voice would have cut diamonds. "How dare you speak so to me?"

Crichton was breathing hard and his cheek muscle twitched. "I speak as is my duty, My Lady."

Color rushed backed into the queen's face, flooding from her neck to her face at being addressed without her royal title. Patrick froze, barely daring to breath for the coming explosion.

A thin smile touched Crichton's lips. "The king shall remain within these walls where he is—"

She broke in, "Where you can control him to increase your own power! I see what you are. I always suspected it. A petty, power-grubbing climber."

Crichton stilled except for that jumping in his cheek. "Whatever you may say of me, I ken my duty to the king and the realm. If you hate this castle so much, so be it. Leave. The king stays." He turned to the guard and said, "Go to the king and see that he is nae disturbed. Keep guard before his door. He is not to leave his chamber until I give permission."

The queen was rigid with rage. She clenched her fists, and for a moment Patrick thought she would strike the man. Her eyes narrowed, and she said softly, "You will pay for this, My Lord, for you've declared yourself my enemy." She spun on her heel, her skirts billowing around her and sailed out of the room. “Ladies, come. We shall prepare to leave for Holyrood."

Patrick sucked in a quick breath and glanced at Lord Gray. The room had grown so silent Crichton's footsteps were a drumbeat as he marched out into the bailey yard. The door slammed and outside he was shouting for his sergeant.

"He... he means to hold the king," Boyd said.

Lord Gray's face was mouth was pressed into a thin line, his brow furrowed. "So it seems."

His father and a few other nobles each had some men-at-arms with them, but the force of Edinburgh Castle might well number near a thousand. And Crichton controlled both entrance and egress. If he chose to hold the king there, especially with the approval of Douglas, no one could stop him.

Patrick stared at the door where the Crichton had exited thinking on the fact that the man had been named chancellor only the day before by the most powerful noble in Scotland. "Can he do that?" he asked.

His father's voice was flat when he replied, "And as long as the Douglas is on Crichton's side? Yes. He can."

Patrick turned his head to star at his father who gave him a pointed look.

"Patrick, your place is with the king. You will do your duty. I must go to the queen."

5

JUNE 1439

It was the first truly hot day of the summer, and the sun was blinding in a clear Edinburgh sky.

The eight year old king was dashing as fast as could, arms and legs furiously pumping, across the stable yard. He slowed a little to give the ball made from a pig's bladder a kick. Three boys in rough hoddin-gray tunics were two yards behind, but they were catching up fast. They were all bigger, and it would be a matter of seconds before they caught up with him. Fergus, the master blacksmith's son, tackled him. They both went rolling. The other two dashed past at a breathless run to kick the ball toward the sticks that were their makeshift goal.

Patrick crossed his arms and leaned a shoulder against the stable wall, thoroughly glad for his charge to be occupied for a while.

James and his attacker were rolling on the ground trading giggling insults. "Big clumsy ox," the king shouted between giggles.

They tussled, rolling in the dirt, as the other boy crowed, "Slow poke that cannae outrun a wean."

"Can too. I can outrun you."

"Nuh uh." The boy sat up and looked around for their mates. The other boys were jumping up and down celebrating their goal.

"Then let's have a race. I bet I can beat you if you dinnae tackle me."

A bellowed shout of "What's to do here?" froze all four of them in place. Crichton swaggered like a bantam rooster into the stable yard to stand over Fergus. He crossed his arms and glared down at the boy who jumped to his feet. "We were only playing at football."

"You laid hands on the king, you insulant pup." Fergus paled at that accusation as the chancellor continued glaring at him. "I should have you whipped within an inch of your life."

James was gaping in open-mouthed horror. "He just tackled me. It's what you do when you play football." He stuck his lower lip out in an impressive pout and clamored to his feet. "You've spoilt our game!"

Crichton thrust a finger at Fergus. "You. Hie you to your father and see that you make yourself useful. I'll have no lads who are wastrels in my castle." He turned to James. "And you. You are a king not some... some ghillie to be rolling in the dirt!"

James glowered at him, looking too angry to continue his pout. "You will nae let me do anything. You won't let me ride my horse or fly my falcon. Now you won't let me play with my friends."

Crichton glanced around until he spotted Patrick. "You. You are supposed to be watching the king. You're to see that the ruffians remember their place. Don't let it happen again."

Patrick stifled a sigh as he straightened and strolled towards the two. "The lad must have some entertainment, My Lord, surely. Mayn't I take him out for a little hunt? With a dozen men-at-arms, there would be no danger."

“I wanted to ride,” King James said with a touch of whine in his voice.

"It is too dangerous. Find him something suitable to do in the castle." He turned on his heel and strode away.

James glared after Crichton. "He's mean and I dinnae like him."

Patrick rubbed his forehead. He had to share the king's feelings, but they'd have to manage. “You'd best keep to games that don't involve roughhousing when you play with your friends—at least when the Chancellor is within the castle."

"Then they probably won't want to play with me anymore then.”

“Remind Fergus that you can beat him in a race, and I think that he will. For now, I need to practice my sword strokes.” He remembered very well his own excitement when he first handed a sword and hoped the young king would feel the same. Besides it was time for him to begin learning. He hid a smile as he continued, “Mayhap Your Grace needs a bit of practice as well?”

James scowled at him. “I dinnae have a sword.”

“Och, then I wonder whose that was that I saw in the armory. It looked exactly your size.”

James's eyes widened. “There is a sword there I could use? Would you teach me?”

“Aye, I suppose I could do that.” He motioned to the armory through a gate past the stable yard. James skipped along with him excitedly as they entered the yard. Above them on the high curtain wall, a man-at-arms walked his rounds. On the opposite side of the dirt-packed yard, two others of Crichton's men traded blows with blunted weapons. Patrick started for the armory, speaking as he walked. “I must find a weapon for practice as well.”

James ran ahead of him. “Haste you. My tutor said I must do lessons later today. I've been hiding from him.”

Patrick lengthened his stride to catch up with his royal charge, smiling at the lad's idea of hiding. Inside the armory, a smith was bent over a bench sharpening a weapon. He gave them a bob of his head before continuing his work. There were bins of weapons, swords hung from hooks on the walls and several bows were racked. Patrick had hunted down the child-sized sword, an excellent one, knowing he’d need to keep the king entertained. Being confined to the castle would have driven any active lad to rebellion, and the king was as hearty and active as any. Patrick was thankful for summer so they could at least spend time in the practice yard. Winter months cooped up with a lad as restless as James was a trial in trying to keep him from breaking his neck as he climbed every height that he could.

Back out in the warm sunlight, Patrick knelt beside James, showed him a good grip on the pommel and let him take a few practice swings. “First, you must learn to parry.” He moved James’ arms so the sword was downward in a guard position, tilting the blade so the edge was at an angle. “You see how you can swing your sword to cover the width of your body?”

Straightening, Patrick demonstrated arcing the blade in a semi-circle before him, so he could catch an incoming weapon. “Like that.”

The young king scowled in concentration as he tried the move in awkward imitation. After a dozen tries, he had a reasonable facsimile of a parry, so Patrick took him to the center of the yard. He gently swung at the king because even with a blunted blade, he could hurt the lad if it landed. Their blades clashed and James managed to catch Patrick’s blade but not quite with the flat as he should. Still it was a start.

After half an hour of showing James how to catch a blade

with his and turn it to lock Patrick's sword, sweat was dripping down James's face. He rubbed his sword arm as though it ached, but he grinned up at Patrick, beaming in satisfaction.

"I have it now," he said.

"Aye, so you do, sire. But we dinnae want to overdo it on your first day. And here is someone I'm thinking from your tutor."

James' grin disappeared when one of the castle servants rushed to them and said, "Your Grace, your tutor awaits your attendance."

"We'll practice more tomorrow," Patrick told him. "And mayhap we can fly your goshawk to a lure. You want him to be used to you when it is safe to hunt."

James dashed for the armory and put away his sword. Patrick had to admit the lad been taught to respect a weapon. Or perhaps it was knowledge that it was lack of a sword at hand that had allowed assassins to slay his father that gave him respect for the blade.

Once the boy king was out of sight, Patrick sauntered toward the castle gates. The sun was its zenith and he was late for where he was expected. In spite of Crichton's constant warnings about danger, the portcullis was raised. Crichton was deep in a quiet conversation with a man-at-arms, but not one of his own men. Patrick kept his face blank when he recognized the red heart on a field scattered with black dots of the Earl of Avondale on the stranger's cloak.

Crichton gave Patrick an inquiring look and asked, "Nae with the king then?"

"He is with his tutor so I dinnae think he needs guarding more than your men provide. They'll nae allow anyone to reach him, and I shall take a bit of time for..." He grinned amiably and shrugged. "...for more amiable company."

Crichton grunted. "I told your father that so young a master of the king's guard would be a bad choice."

"Sir, William, if you think it is too dangerous for the king to bide alone with his tutor then I shall stay. I may be young, but my duty comes first." Patrick wondered what he would have to do for the man to warm to him, but he wouldn't give up.

"No, no. The king is safe with his tutor, but remember that your duties as a gentleman of the bedchamber come before wenching."

Patrick's face heated but he bowed. Under the shadow of the massive stone barbican that guarded the gates, Patrick looked back. Once more Crichton was in close conversation with the stranger.

He walked down the hill and onto Edinburgh's busy High Street, through the raucous noise of the market where merchants and shoppers argued and shouted over prices and quality of the goods on sale. Overhead a flock of white-winged gannets turned, calling out their harsh "krak krak krak".

Patrick looked about as he strolled, stopping to examine a dirk and glanced behind. No one seemed to be following him. He kept his head down when a troop of men clattered past, more men with the Earl of Avondale's colors on their surcoats. *What were the men of Douglas of Avondale doing in Edinburgh?* He waited until no one he recognized was in sight. A burly laborer with faggots tied on his back cursed him freely as a useless noble git for impeding his path.

The lodging Patrick sought lay down a nameless vennel off High Street. Although he saw no sign of being followed, Patrick picked his way down the shadowy alley with some caution. The shutters of the house were closed, but the mumble of men's voices carried through the slats. Patrick followed the sound and knocked on the door. It was opened by a man in a Benedictine's white robe and black cloak.

"Sir?"

A loud voice commanded, "It's Sir Patrick. Let him enter."

Inside, James Kennedy, now Bishop of Dunkeld, lean as ever, his short beard neatly trimmed, and tonsured, was waiting in the shuttered room, seated on a folding chair with a stand of half-burnt candles and a flagon of wine on a table beside him. Patrick's father was peering through the slats of the shutter with his back to them. The hearth was empty because of the day's warmth and only a couple of stools took up the rest of the room. The candle light gleamed on the purple brocade of the bishop's gown and the silver fittings of his scrip hanging from his ornate belt.

He held out his hand, and Patrick knelt to kiss his ring. "I want a full account of what has been happening at the castle."

Patrick murmured an assent.

"You kept us waiting," Lord Gray said.

"I came as soon as my duties with his grace allowed," Patrick parried. His father always accused him of keeping him waiting.

Kennedy gestured and Patrick took a seat on the nearby stool. He gave a succinct account of the king's activities, being close confined to the castle, and that Crichton still had not warmed to him. He paused. The two men of state, absorbed but unrevealing, watched him as he spoke. Lord Gray poured himself a cup of wine and then turned to stare out onto the vennel again.

Patrick concluded with the news that they would be most interested to hear. "But he has been in close contact with Douglas of Avondale. Just today there was a man-at-arms in the earl's colors who must have been carrying messages, and a troop of the earl's men passed as I came here."

"You have not heard, then, what the messages said."

Patrick shook his head. "I am not privy to that. He makes sure not to discuss anything important in my hearing. I've managed a few glimpses of letters that were nothing except orders for managing his lands"

Kennedy propped his elbows on the table and rubbed his forehead, lost in thought for a moment. "I am surprised the news has nae been noised about yet but no doubt that is what the message was. Things are going to come to a head soon and if Creighton...." He shook his head. "I must think on this."

Patrick looked from the bishop to his father's stiff back. "What news?"

"The Earl of Douglas is dead," his father said without turning.

"What? How?" Patrick's mind reeled. "Was there a battle?"

"He was on his way to his castle at Threave and died near Restalrig. Of a fever." Lord Gray made a noise in his throat. "This changes everything. The new earl is but a lad."

"When did it happen?"

Kennedy wove his fingers together. "Three days ago. Soon the word will be everywhere that the Lieutenant General of Scotland is dead."

Patrick leaned back, mind darting. "Crichton?"

"Is weakened," Lord Gray said. "And now may be the time to act, though whether the plan is wise? I believe not."

"It is the Queen's plan, whether wise or not. And in the power void with a child the Earl of Douglas, now is the perfect time to act." Kennedy slapped his hand onto the table. "Did Crichton think such a woman as Queen Joan, who stood up to assassins who came for her husband and then had them executed before her very eyes, would stand by and see her son stolen? He misjudged badly if he did."

"Hardly stolen," Lord Gray protested. "She left him in Crichton's care, though unwillingly. But, aye, for two years she has seethed at being slighted and insulted. So now there is this scheme."

"Scheme, sir?" The word did not bode well.

"One in which you have a part to play. But for the nonce, all you must ken is that on the morrow, the queen will arrive with two of her daughters, her ladies, and a small company."

"But..." Patrick stumbled over his words, too taken aback to know what to ask. "But she was furious with Crichton when he insisted the king must bide in Edinburgh Castle. She is just going to come back?" To meekly suffer an insult was nothing like the woman he had had seen at Robert Stewart's execution.

"She means to make peace with Crichton. She will plead a widow's grief for her harsh words and assure him that she now believes he is in the right to keep the king with him for...safety."

"But?"

"But for now, do anything you can to assure Crichton that you believe her. Having her visit the king will surely make his care easier. You say he is a restless boy, not easy to handle. A visit from his mother and sisters will distract him."

Patrick snorted. "Not that he pays the lad much mind, except to shout at him to act like a king."

"Possibly more than you ken. Having the king in his care is what gives him any power he has, after all."

Patrick looked at his father, confused.

"With the earl's death our position is much strengthened with the new earl little more than a lad himself, barely in his fifteenth year. But as long as Crichton has the king in his possession, he cannot be touched. He can hatch whatever plots will increase his power."

"Aye, I remember young Douglas from the coronation. He and his brother accompanied the earl. So what is my part in this scheme? Only to convince Crichton of the queen's sincerity?"

"As I said, for the nonce, do nothing" said Kennedy. "Once the queen has arrived and Crichton is reassured, then we shall see how to restore the king to his mother."

Lord Gray shook his head and opened the shutter a crack. He peered out onto the alley. Obviously he was not confident in this plan to regain the king, whatever it was. Kennedy had the name of a canny man, yet something about the plan had his lord father uneasy. But the death of the Earl of Douglas had thrown power up in the air like blowing leaves. How knew where the power would land? Having the king in their hands would make those leaves blow their way.

"Aye," Kennedy said thoughtfully. "You are not to let on that you kent the queen would arrive. He will no doubt question you on it. Mayhap if you first express some doubt of her intent and then reassure him of her sincerity after seeing her with her son, that would help convince him."

"I shall do what I can," Patrick said.

Kennedy nodded. "I shan't risk returning while she is here. Once it is dark, I shall ride for Leith to await news. The queen will have your further commands. I must leave for Bologna within the week, so I trust you to follow the queen's commands."

Dismissed, Patrick stood. "For Bologna?"

"Aye, Pope Eugene will invest me in my bishopric there." He smiled with satisfaction. "Be assured, I'll nae tarry longer than I must. But with war with the antipope raging across Europe, this trip is vital. However serious the situation is here, I must openly show my loyalty to the rightful pope and being invested by him will increase my influence here as well."

Bowing, Patrick mulled over how much this newly acquired office would increase Kennedy's power and possibly the Queen's. Dunkeld was not the most powerful bishopric in

Scotland, but Cameron had lost much power. He silently walked out of house followed by his father who caught him by the arm, studying him with dark eyes. “We’re taking a great risk. Be careful.”

“Certes, My Lord.” Then he thought of something that his father and Kennedy should know. “Och, whatever it was that Crichton was discussing with Avondale's man, they were at pains not to be overheard. Would he have bothered if it was the Earl of Douglas's death? That news will soon be abroad anyroad.”

Lord Gray shrugged. "Avondale is not powerful enough to be a concern." He turned to reenter the house, but paused. “And the king? Is he tractable? Will persuading him to do as he as telt be a problem?”

“If he is told it is an adventure, he will cooperate willingly, but he is no meek lad. As you would expect of his father’s son.”

“Aye?” He tapped his chin with a finger thoughtfully. A ring flashed as his hand moved. “I think you will be able to convince him that it is an adventure.”

The door shut in Patrick's face. He stood stock still for a moment before he pinched the bridge of his nose, the throb against the throb of a headache. Why had his father thought he would be a good spy?

6

By midday Patrick felt some sense of achievement. He and Alex Boyd had spent an hour tending their armor. Patrick wiped and oiled his neglected breast piece and found his mislaid gorget. King James had wearied of watching the two work, so he slashed about with his new blade until he was briskly told it was no toy. Patrick stopped what he was doing to fashion a wooden sword for him with a couple of scraps of wood, so the lad went back to dancing about, hacking and slashing at an invisible enemy. Patrick wondered if the enemy was Crichton.

They cleaned the tack for their coursers, which job neither trusted to the stable hands. Once finished with that, Patrick sat down astride a long bench with a whetstone in front of him, wet it, and carefully worked the sword back and forth to bring it to a perfect edge. James sporadically practiced the parry Patrick had taught him interspersed with wild swings and shouts as he defeated his foe.

Patrick had just returned his blade to the scabbard at his side when Alexander Lyon, who was officially a member of the king's household though seldom in attendance, hurried into the practice yard. Behind him, Patrick heard distant shouting, the beat of a drum and, a trumpet's fanfare. "There's a procession coming up the Via Royale," he said excitedly. "A group of horses with men-at-arms in royal livery under the royal banner."

"The royal banner?" Alex Boyd frowned with a confused look. "But that would have to be the queen."

James dropped his toy sword. "My lady mother? Hurry. Let's go see if it truly is her!"

By the time they reached the gate, the outriders had already entered the bailey yard; the drum and trumpet had fallen silent. They were followed by a small but richly dressed cavalcade, silks shimmering in the noonday sun, jewels gleaming, horses draped in dyed leather. The people of Edinburgh had followed to stand outside the walls, some cheering. There were a few shouts of "Queen Joan!" and "Hurrah for the Queen!"

The trumpeter blew another blast as the queen came to a stop in the middle of the bailey. James pointed. "Look! Isabella and Mary are with her." James had never said that he missed his numerous sisters, but being from such a large family, he must have. And now his eyes gleamed with excitement as he bounced on his toes.

Boyd nudged Patrick with his shoulder. He dipped his head toward a distinguished-looking Augustinian monk in a black cassock whose beard hung down onto his chest. "I think that's David White, the Abbot of Cambuskenneth Abbey. I saw him at the coronation. But who is that with him?"

Beside the monk rode a dark-haired man who looked perhaps about forty, with a three starred badge on his cloak. "One of the Douglases, without doubt with that badge." Alexander Lyon put in.

"But which one?" Alex Boyd asked as the man dismounted

and strode to take one of her hand with a flourish and bowed so she could step onto his other hand and dismount.

Patrick leaned close to Alex Boyd and said softly, "I saw him at the coronation with. That's the Black Knight of Lorne, Sir James Stewart." He pointed. "And I think that's Sir William, his brother, with them."

The door of the keep was flung open and Crichton stamped down the steps toward the queen's party, his face wrinkled into a scowl like a withered apple.

"Come on!" James was nearly dancing with excitement. "I must go greet them."

Patrick looked from the boy king to the queen to the angry-looking nobleman stalking toward her. He was at a loss of the proper course of action. Well, the lad did have to greet his mother. It was only fitting, but he could only pray this did not go as astray as it might.

"Aye, you're right, sire. You must greet your lady mother." He shrugged at Alex Boyd. "Like a gentleman, Your Grace," he called after the king who was dashing full tilt across the bailey.

Queen Joan stepped toward Crichton and held out both of her hands. "Sir, I regret that angry look you are giving me and fear that I deserve it. We parted with such bitter words between us. They were my fault." She sighed. "I hope you will remember that I was grieving for my husband and king, and in no state of mind to be sensible about your care for my son. But I give you may oath, I know that you only desire his wellbeing."

Patrick swallowed down a grin as Crichton blinked, his expression changing from furious to confused. He opened his mouth. He closed it. He looked at the queen's still extended hands and then up at her smiling face.

If her waist might have thickened with childbearing and a few lines at her eyes, she was a still beautiful woman. No one had ever wondered that she had captured the heart of the late king. She would be a hard woman to resist when she turned her wide blue eyes on a man.

Crichton's expression softened. He took both her hands and bowed to kiss each. "Your Grace." He cleared his throat. "Certes, I ken that you were grieving for the late king. I..." He cleared his throat again. "You are most welcome at Edinburgh Castle and your company as well." His tone turned waspish when he continued. "It is a pity I did nae have a chance to prepare for your arrival."

"Mother!" James shouted as he reached her.

The Queen laughed as she hugged James. "Manners, Your Grace. Is that any proper way to greet me?"

She released him so he could bow. "My lady mother, I am so happy to see you!"

The Black Knight of Lorne had already helped fourteen year old Isabella and twelve-year old Mary from their horses. Mary hurried over calling, "Brother." Isabella was on her dignity following more sedately.

When Sir James joined them, Crichton eyed him coldly. "Sir James. You keep well, I hope." His tone would have indicated he hoped otherwise.

"I do, sir. And keep even better now that we bring our queen together with her son." He smiled.

Crichton glowered, but Queen Joanna interrupted by extending putting her hand on Crichton's arm. "I am sure we will all be much more comfortable inside, Sir William. After our ride I thirst and I would love to hear all the news of my son. He's always been a vigorous lad, so I hope he's not given you trouble."

Whether he was totally convinced by the queen's words or not, Crichton had no choice but turn to lead the whole procession up the few steps and through the doorway into the Great Hall.

"Sir Patrick is teaching me to use a sword," James prattled on. "We practiced and practiced. I'm sure I'm going to be gey good."

"Are you? That is fine news." She gave Patrick an approving smile.

Servants scuttled around the room lighting candles. The hall smelled of lavender and thyme mixed into the rushes. Crichton escorted the queen to a seat at the trestle table on the dais. He turned over a stack of parchment so the writing did not show and called for flagons of wine. "My lady, be welcome. And all of you lords and ladies. The trip must have been wearisome coming from Scone, I ken. Please all, be seated."

When the queen was seated, Crichton took a place beside her

Patrick took a seat at the end of the table and saw her share a smile with the Black Knight of Lorne. *He is gey bonnie, and she is a widow*. But he dismissed the thought as foolishness. She was also a queen. When Lady Annabella sat beside him, he filled her cup. She looked him in the eye with surprising directness. She had blue eyes, as blue as Loch Lomond, frank and searching, yet there was something spirited in them as well. Her eyes and the rest of her were enough to make a man's heart beat faster and his had begun to hammer alarmingly. But she was a member of the queen's household and this was not time to chance giving offense.

At the opposite end of the table Lady Janet silently watched the queen.

James leaned on the arm of his mother's chair and gave her what Patrick recognized as his most wheedling smile. "I've been flying my hawk, too. But the best is practicing my sword. May I show you it? May I?"

"You may show me later, but your sisters might like to see your sword and your hawk. Why don't you ask?"

Isabella looked less than enthusiastic, but Mary nodded happily. The two agreed to go with James to see his treasures. Patrick had to chuckle as James's chatter to his sisters was cut off by the closing of the door.

Queen Joanna sipped her wine and then sadly shook her head. "I mislike to mention sad news, but the death of Earl Archibald hit me very hard. He was such a good friend of my lord husband." She wrung he hands. "And now we have no lieutenant general of the kingdom."

Crichton's eyes narrowed. "Let us be frank. Is that why you are here? What is it you would have of me, my lady?"

"Why naught, sir, except your continued guarding of my dear son." She fixed the man with an amused look. "I would merely spend a little time with him. I have missed him so."

"A woman longs for her children," the Black Knight said brusquely. "There is nothing more natural."

"Surely such a small party as ours is no threat to this great castle," Sir William Stewart said. "We can hardly besiege you and steal the lad. Although tomorrow I hope you'll allow us to borrow some birds. I have a taste for hawking."

"And desire to take the lad with you," Crichton barked. "I shall nae allow it."

Sir William put his hands up and laughed. "By the saints, man. I thought you might like to join us. We'll make it a hunting party of us men and leave the ladies to enjoy the children's prattle." He raised his eyebrows at his older brother. "You'd join us for hawking, would you not, brother. The weather is fine for it."

The abbot smiled as he took a sip of his wine. "I have had enough riding. A quiet day in the solar and a tour of the Royal Chapel would suit me better."

"Aye." Sir James gave Crichton a wicked grin. "If we are all friends it will ease everyone's minds. We're nae well acquainted, sir, so we can mend that whilst the queen spends time with her son. Surely you have nae worry that she'll hie off with him whilst we are away."

"You mustn't fash Lord Crichton so," the queen scolded. "I fear I gave him reason for his distrust, but I doubt he wants to stay with me while I listen to the king tells me about his hawks and his sword. I'd have him read to me so I can see how his studies progress." She chuckled. "It's a pastime a mother will love, but I doubt it appeals to fine knights such as the lot of you."

Crichton's smile was closer to a grimace. "Certes, I dinnae think the queen would steal off alone with her son, but I have business I must see to. The hawking is good near here, and you are more than welcome to enjoy it."

Patrick bit his lip trying to decide what he should do if the queen's party split up. If he rode with the men, they would be free to give him directions, but perhaps the queen wanted to do so herself. "Mayhap I would be in your way spending time with the king."

She glanced Patrick's way and said in a mild tone, "I would love to watch whilst you give him one of these famous lessons in swordsmanship, Sir Patrick. Please do stay."

He inclined his head. "As it please Your Grace."

"I fear the king has outgrown needing his mother at hand. Such is the fate of all mothers." She sighed. "I have never been fond of this castle. It is a dour place, but safe. Sir Crichton has the right of that."

Crichton nodded. "I see to it that our king is never at risk."

"We trust you entirely, sir." She tapped her chin with a finger. "I believe I may not return often. Whilst I am here, I shall have my ladies pack the clothing I have yet here and some bed hangings I'm quite fond of."

"Och, if you like."

"You are too kind, Lord Crichton. Thank you." She smiled

sweetly and hid a yawn behind her hand. "I must needs rest, I fear. The long ride left me weary."

The Black Knight snorted. "Women. 'Tis always something. If we're to return with the Queen's finery, it's best I arrange another wagon. The one we have with us will hardly suffice. And I would check to be sure the animals are properly stabled."

His brother muttered something about accompanying him and the two men rose. Patrick bowed to the queen as she and her ladies strolled to the doorway leading to the stairs to the upper floors. He started to follow the other men, but Crichton said, "Sir Patrick."

"Aye, My Lord?" He turned to where Crichton, still seated on the dais.

Crichton tapped his forefinger on the table, looking pensive, for several moments before he spoke. "Did you ken that the queen would be arriving?"

Patrick longed for more practice in acting. He was improving, at least. "I did nae, sir. I have had nae messages from her grace since though I have sent her several letters that I showed you, assuring her of the king's wellbeing. In fact—" He broke off and bit his lip.

"In fact?" Crichton prompted impatiently.

"I was surprised. She is... How should I say it? Proud?" He nodded. "Aye, she is a proud woman, as she should be certes, so returning to tell you she was in the wrong surprised me. But it is a good thing, surely? It will be better if there is agreement between the king's chancellor and his mother."

"So you believe that she is content for the king to remain here in my care."

Patrick widened his eyes, unsure how well he did innocent. "She has no choice. I doubt it pleases her, but mending her quarrel with you allows her to visit from time to time. That is for the best, dinnae you think?"

Crichton grunted noncommittally and stroked his short beard. "Aye. I suppose. And I suppose you have duties to attend."

"Indeed. I had best see that the king hasn't absconded with one of the sharpened swords." He sauntered to the door, but the back of his neck itched from Crichton's stare.

First, he had better indeed see where the king had made off to and that he had not found mischief to lead his sisters into. James's fondness for finding somewhere high to perch was alarming, but Patrick found the three of them in the lower bailey throwing a ball for one of the castle's pups. That seemed safe enough.

Now he only had to reach the queen's chambers in David's Tower without Crichton knowing. That could not be seen from the great hall where he'd left the chancellor, but had he remained?

Strolling casually back the way he came, he passed the doors to the great hall. He opened the left hand door and entered. The ceiling rose up two stories, not as high as that of the great hall but it was still impressively vaulted. One of the servants was replacing candles to be lit later if needed, climbing a ladder to reach holders a full eight feet off the floor. Two women were freshening the rushes by strewing dried lavender. A few children were playing a hiding game behind the large columns. A man-at-arms stood guard at the foot of the stairs.

Patrick nodded casually to the guard and started to climb. The man was certain to report he had been here, curse it. He would simply have to make up a story to cover his presence. Even in the daytime the stairs were dark with only a few stray shafts of light from narrow windows. He made his way up three stories to where he knew the queen's solar was, hoping that was where he would find her.

The door was closed and he gave a soft knock. The voice of Sir James Stewart told him to enter.

Annabella stood looking at an extremely large kist, frowning. But the queen held out her hands to Patrick and smiled. "Sir Patrick."

He closed the door and bent to kiss her hand. When he straightened he saw that Sir James shared Annabella's frown, but his was directed at Patrick. He started to speak and then his frown deepened.

Patrick turned and went back to the door, opened it and checked in both directions to be sure no one was near. He closed it softly and said to Queen Joan, "Bishop Kennedy commanded me to aid you in any way that I can, Your Grace, but I give you my word, I needed no such command. If I can aid you, I shall."

Her smiled broadened, and she slid a triumphant glance at Sir James. "I told you as much, did I not?"

"This must be secret," Sir James said, still frowning. "Entirely secret. You swear on your honor that you'll nae reveal it?"

Patrick flushed with indignation, but he still said, “By Saint Patrick and all the saints, I swear I would never betray the queen nor the bishop."

Sir James merely nodded and turned as Annabella knelt and opened the kist. "It is large enough, Your Grace, but..." The queen and Sir James went to look into the kist as Annabella pulled out a long blue silk gown. Shoes and several headdresses followed.

"Aye, it will do. I was sure it would," the queen said.

Patrick stared at the three of them in bafflement. "Do what?"

Then Sir James looked at him and actually laughed. "It is for transporting a most royal cargo."

Queen Joan put her hand on his arm and squeezed. "Hush. You must not tease about it."

In bafflement, Patrick looked at each of them in turn.

"Here is the plan." The queen's smile faded into a look of solemn determination. "In this kist, I had stored some of my clothing and bedding the last time I was at the castle. I will tell Crichton that I shall remove my belongings so he may have free use of the solar if he likes. That he will welcome, no doubt. Then all my clothing will be removed, hidden somewhere, the kist well-padded with blankets for comfort, and the king will hide himself inside. It has a good lock so there is no danger of it being opened. We acquired a good cart on our way. Sir James will pretend to bring it to suit my whim for my clothes. We shall have men-at-arms carry the kist down. Then we are away."

Patrick almost choked. "Your Grace! Hide the king in a kist?" He realized his voice had squeaked like a lad's and cleared his throat.

"We will pad it well with good blankets. No harm will come to him, and if he's like most lads he'll think it's a fine adventure," Sir James said.

Annabella, still kneeling by the kist, had watched the to and fro like a tennis match. "It is large enough. Come look, Sir Patrick."

She smiled up at him and the way her eyes gleamed, Patrick wondered if she thought it was a fine adventure as well. He went to squat next to the kist and closed the lid. Then he opened it again. "Aye, it is large enough for the lad, but what if aught should happen, something unexpected, and you are delayed letting him out? It is tightly fitted. He could die from not having enough air."

Lady Annabella put her hand on his arm. "Och, that is a good thought. We must find a way to let air into the kist."

Sir James let out a low "hmmmm" as he stood over them.

The queen paced slowly around the kist frowning at it. "But surely we will not be delayed, so there will be no danger."

Patrick shook his head. "There is always a chance of delay. You will nae want to let him out until you are on the other side of the Forth." He rubbed his chin beard. "There must be some way to let in air."

While they spoke, Annabella took out more neatly folded clothes from the kist. They were brightly colored, lovely rose colored and blue and green, in shimmering silk and lush velvet.

"If we put any holes in it, they will show as raw wood," Sir James said. "That would nae work."

Patrick closed the lid again and examined the hinges. "Look. The hinges are broad and heavy. If we carve the wood behind them out, the hinge would hide the damage. We should be able to make large enough holes that it will let in enough air. Especially since the kist is so large."

Annabella bit her lip. She opened the kist, closed it and opened it again. "Mayhap a small opening behind the clasp in the front, as well. The clasp would hide it." She gave Patrick an intent look. "We must take nae chances."

"Aye, but who can do it? We cannot possibly trust anyone here to work on it," Queen Joan said.

"I shall do it myself. I'll sneak a tool from the carpentry tonight." Yet more sneaking. "Then I will come here and have it done before morning."

Patrick frowned as another problem occurred to him. "What about me and the rest of the king's household? If we left with you, it would give the game away."

"I dinnae think that is such a problem," the Sir James said. "You must stay behind. Take leave of the queen in the bailey, and then go about your business. When it is discovered the king is gone, you must be distressed and insulted that you were nae tellt. When we reach Stirling Castle, we will send word that the king is safe and in good hands and command that you and the others join us there."

Patrick sucked on his front teeth as he considered the plan. He did not like it, but could think of no other. "Och, I suppose that is for the best. But how long do you plan to stay? He questioned me whether I'd kent you were coming. He is suspicious yet."

The queen's mouth pressed into an angry line. "We must stay at least a few days. He has no claim to hold the king, and he shall not. But he must suspect nothing."

The Black Knight took her hand and kissed it. "You will charm him as you do everyone, My Queen. He will nae suspect a thing."

7

Patrick nudged the door closed with an elbow since both hands were full. He sat a stand with three lit candles onto the floor. A glance showed that that the shutters were closed, so the faint light should attract no attention. He hunkered in front of the kist and glanced at the tool in his hand. He had seen the carpenters use such to make holes, It was an odd looking thing they called a brace, but as long as it worked he cared not what it was called. The fact was, he'd never before even had reason to touch such things.

He put the tool, with its long bent wooden handle and sharp twisted metal point, on the floor and rubbed his hands up and down his thighs. Slowly, he opened the kist and ran his fingers over the places where he needed to make air holes. This couldn't be too difficult surely, but he wished he could have brought a carpenter to do the job. A carpenter would have had some clue what he was doing. After darting a glance at the closed door, he picked up the tool, wishing fervently that the queen had trusted this to almost anyone else.

Behind the hinge in the back would probably be less noticeable if he somehow messed it up. He pressed the sharp point against the inside edge of the kist, leaning into the tool. The kist slid and Patrick slipped, catching himself to keep from tumbling inside. He cursed, and pushed himself upright. Of course, he had to put the chest where it was braced. *Stupid.*

He dropped the tool inside and shoved the kist, the rug it sat upon going with it, until it was backed against the wall. Wiping his brow with his forearm, he let out a long breath. He could do this and would do so if it took him all night. A click when the door was opened made him jump to his feet, his heart galloping in his chest. He spun and Annabella slipped in through the partially opened door.

"Mother of God, Lady Annabella, what are you doing here?" he burst out. Then he realized he had spoken so loudly someone might have heard. Blood rushed to his cheeks and he whispered, "I didnae mean to shout." He went past her to the door, and opened it a crack to peek out and then stuck his head out to look in both directions. The light from a torch flickered on the stairway but all was silent with not even the sound of a footfall. He closed the door and leaned on it for a moment.

She put a hand on his arm. "I'm sorry to give you a start, Sir Patrick. I could nae sleep so I just came to see..." She nodded toward the kist.

He turned to look at her curiously; he was surprised that she was brave enough to wander the castle alone at night. She gave him a level look and the curve of her lips made him smile. She was doe-eyed and slim but he wondered how she got those freckles across her very straight nose. For warmth, she was wrapped snuggly in a long plaid checked green and yellow for warmth over her white linen kirtle.

"I am only now starting. First, I needed to find a tool to make the holes with." He knelt back down at the kist and picked up the brace. "I've seen carpenters use this to make holes, so I am sure that I can as well." He frowned down at the tool in his hands, trying to picture exactly how he had seen it used.

Her kirtle whispered about her feet as she came to kneel beside him. "That is a very strange looking thing."

"Aye." He blew out a breath and did his best to demonstrate how he was pretty sure it was used. "You put the point where you need the hole and then you..." He grasped the bent portion of the handle which should have spun the point. It wobbled so he leant onto it. That made it bite into the wood and steadied it, so he could turn it and turn it.

"It's working," she whispered.

"Aye." Her arm was warm as she leaned close, and she had a soft scent of roses.

He kept his eyes firmly on the hole that was forming as he turned the brace. He pretended that the sweat that broke out on his brow was from exertion, but truth, it was nerves. Every second, he expected one of Crichton's men-at-arms to come through the door. After minutes turning, the point of the tool broke through to the other side. When he pulled it out, the wood splintered. He drew his dirk and worked the splintered bits loose for a larger hole. He pried until it was a carved notch in the top rim of the kist about the width of his thumb.

Annabella brushed the wood fragments away. He cut his glance toward her and she was beaming. "It worked," she whispered.

"Aye, but 'tis nae large enough. I think if I make another just next to it, I can make it larger. I think that will be big enough to let in air, to be safe."

"Is one hole enough?"

He chewed his lip for a moment. "Let us see how it looks once I'm done. If it does nae show, then I think you were right. I should make another in the front, but that one I'll only drill through once. It would be easier to see I'm afeart."

"I cannot believe that you were able to do this," she said.

He felt his face get hot. "I ken it is nae skill for a knight, but I'll do whatever I must for the king."

"But it's wonderful that you have. 'Tis noble of you. And I begin to believe that we will get him away." She turned and grasped his forearm. "We must. It is a terrible thing to keep him here when he should be with his mother and his sisters. Truly, I believe that."

"Wheesht." He was glad the light was faint so she wouldn't see that he was blushing. "'Tis nothing noble about making a hole in a kist."

She laughed softly. "But I think there is."

The drilling went faster in the second hole, and then a little prying with his dirk turned it into a large enough space to let in air for the little king. He brushed the saw dust and shards of wood into his hand.

Anabella held out her hand. "Let me." She took them to the window, opened it a sliver, and tossed them into the wind.

Patrick nodded his approval before he turned back to the kist. "I want to see how it looks with the kist closed." He put down the lid and turned it around. She brought the candle and together they examined the hinge that hid the air hole. "I don't see anything. It does nae show at all."

Patrick tugged at his tuft of a beard. "Aye. It will do." One more hole and he would be done, and he could hope he would never have such a task laid to him again. So he opened the kist, looked at the front, and drilled a hole above the metal loop just where the hasp would hide it when it was locked. Once more Annabella disposed of the bits of wood out the window.

Patrick said, "I'll have to find blankets to line it and to soften the inside."

Annabella drew herself up and it was then Patrick realized how petite she was. The top of her head barely came to his chin. "Aye, we must do that. I have coverlets in my chamber, ones stuffed with feathers that will be very soft for him. There's no time to lose. Let us go."

Patrick wondered what he should say as he followed her up the stairs to the next story where the queen and her ladies had their chambers. As much as he enjoyed her company, there was a danger that someone would see them together. They could not call attention to themselves now, and being with her in the middle of the night would be a terrible scandal. It would be an even worse scandal and she would be banished from the queen's service if he were caught in her chamber. He leaned close to be sure no one else could hear. "If you bring me the coverlet here, I shall take it down. There is nae reason for you to risk..."

"You think I should nae have risked a scandal." She gave him a rueful smile. "The queen would understand. I only wish to be sure our wee king makes his escape."

Patrick nodded, trying to think of something to assure her of his regard, but nothing came to him. His mind was aswirl with burgeoning desire. Here he was alone with her in the near dark.

Annabella took a step toward him. Her eyes were suddenly downcast and her lips parted, trembling a little. She whispered, "Sir Patrick, there is no one here to see..."

He put his hands on her small waist and leant his face to hers. She raised her hands to his chest.

Their lips touched.

Then she spun away and darted into her room, as he looked after her, his head spinning. He rubbed the back of his neck and ordered his heart not to pound so. In a moment, she returned and thrust a thick feather filled coverlet into his arms. Then she smiled up at him. "Good night," she whispered and the door closed behind her.

The king huffed angrily. "While my mother is here I should nae have to have lessons."

Alex Boyd, kneeling before the king, put the boy's shoes on his feet and stood. "Mayhap, Your Grace, but I dinnae think that is for Sir Patrick or me to decide."

The lad pouted but there was a gleam laughter in his eyes. "I shall talk to my lady mother. I am sure she wants to see me fly my falcon."

Patrick chuckled and clapped Alex on the shoulder. "Go on. I'll see his grace to his tutor."

"Drag him you mean." Alex walked out the door, laughing.

Patrick closed it softly and put his fingers to his lips. He waited a full minute before he checked into the hallway to be sure no one was within sight. He motioned to the king and hurried to the far side of the box bed with its heavy hangings. He grasped the boy's arm, pulled him close and said, "There is a secret, but you must say nothing."

James looked up at him with wide-eyed eagerness. "What? I will nae tell."

"Wheesht. This will be a huge adventure, like..." He thought desperately, trying to remember what heroic tales the lad might have read. "...almost like the tale of the champion Fierabras. People will talk about it for ages, but if Lord Crichton learns it will spoil everything." Patrick glanced nervously toward the door. "You are going to escape from the castle. In hiding."

James bounced with excitement. "With my lady mother? And the others?"

"We must be very careful not to give our plan away. I'll

show you how you'll escape, so you can be ready, but then we must act as though everything is as usual. If Crichton even suspects we have a plan, you ken that it will all be spoilt."

"Show me!" He grabbed Patrick's arm and tugged him toward the door. "I want to see now."

Patrick gently put his hands on the lad's shoulders and turned him. He crouched and looked him intently in the face. "Softly, My King. If Crichton or his men see that you are overwrought, they'll ken something is afoot. This is very important. Your lady mother is counting on you to be calm. This is an adventure, but it is no game."

His young king took a deep breath. His color was still high, eyes shining with excitement, but he nodded solemnly. "I will be very calm. I promise."

"Aye." Patrick had to smile at his earnest expression. "And you always keep your promises. Now I'll show you how you will escape."

No one would think a thing about the king going into the queen's solar to give her a good morning greeting, so he led James boldly past a servant scrubbing the floor and another carrying a load of faggots up the stairs. When he closed the door to the solar, James couldn't contain himself any more. "What? How can I escape in here?" he whispered loudly.

"Look." Patrick lifted the lid. "I made holes, you see, to be sure there would be enough air. And Lord Crichton agreed that your lady mother should take with her the clothing that was still stored here. But instead of clothing, it will be—"

"Me!" James was already climbing in.

"Aye. It is well padded but may still be bumpy when they are moving it. So you must be sure to make no noise, not even a peep, even if you are knocked about or bruised a bit."

James stretched out full length in the kist. "Pffft. You ken I dinnae care about bruises." He pulled back a sleeve and proudly displayed a yellowing bruise from one of his recent tumbles. "I shall be quiet as can be. Like King Robert the Great hiding in a cave." He grinned with obvious satisfaction. "And I'll escape the cruel lord who is holding me prisoner."

Patrick shook his head. Sometimes he thought he saw so clearly the man the young king would become and wondered if Crichton even knew what a fierce enemy was in the making. But there was no point in worrying about it now. His job was to be sure James was prepared for the escape. "I'll close the lid for a moment, so you'll ken what it is going to be like."

"Aye! Close it."

Patrick lowered the lid. "It will be very dark, but the holes will let in air. You can do it, Your Grace, aye?"

"Of course."

Even muffled from within the kist Patrick could hear the scorn. He lifted the lid. "Of course, Your Grace. It will be locked after you're inside to be sure it does nae accidentally come open. They'll carry it down and put it on one of the carts, and then you'll go to a waiting ferry to cross the Forth. They will let you out once you cross, and then on to Stirling Castle with your mother and sisters."

"And Sir James and his brother and the men-at-arms."

Patrick chuckled. "Aye, with them as well."

Then James looked thoughtful. "But what about you? And Alex Boyd?"

"We must stay behind for a while or he would certainly ken that something was wrong. But later, I'll join you. As soon as I can."

James thought that over for a bit. "You are supposed to stay with me to guard me. To keep me safe."

"Sir James will act in my stead. But I shall join you soon. I give you my oath."

Satisfied at last, the king agreed to practice his archery for a while but Patrick agreed that they should ask his sisters to come to, James declaring that even lasses could use a bow as long as it was not too strong a one.

It took two more days before the queen was convinced that Lord Crichton's suspicions were eased. It took a good deal of finesse to keep the king busy and away from the Chancellor, because anyone who paid the slightest attention would soon see that the boy was full of excitement that grew by the hour. He kept his oath and said not a word, but squashing his excitement was beyond him. Patrick was reminded of an exuberant puppy as the boy squirmed, laughed and dashed from archery to falconry to racing his friends to scaling every dangerous spot he could find.

At last the morning of departure arrived. In the outer bailey, everything was abustle. The two wagons were being loaded. Men-at-arms shouted. Horses were saddled and led from the stables. A sharp wind was blowing and whipping the banner above the gate, one the royal lion banner that announced the king was in residence and the other of Lord Crichton.

The Black Knight was in the midst of it shouting commands, eager to be off, the queen and her two daughters watching with Lord Crichton. Patrick walked with the grinning king. "Your Grace." He bowed to the queen mother. "The king wanted to wish you God speed once more."

James rushed to throw his arms around her, "Aye, My Lady Mother, God speed." There was a distinct chortle in his voice.

The queen put her hands on his shoulders and gently disentangled him. "I shall visit you again soon. Work hard on your studies and do not neglect your prayers, Your Grace." She glanced at Sir James. "They have not yet brought down the chest from the solar. Would you and Patrick check on it? James might want to keep you company."

"Of course, Your Grace." He bowed to the king. "After you, sire."

James dashed ahead of them. Patrick would have sworn his stomach was filled with live eels, it roiled so. By the time the two of them reached the solar, James had already climbed inside. He sat giggling.

"Wheesht. Remember you must be quiet as a church mouse, Your Grace." Patrick nodded to Sir James. "Lock it whilst I summon some men-at-arms to carry it."

There were two men-at-arms downstairs in the hall, so Patrick called them to come help. They grumbled that it was not their job to carry things about, but they tromped up the stairs to the solar. "It looks gey heavy," one grumbled.

"Clothing and bedding should nae be that heavy. If you cannot manage, I shall call more men."

With one in the front and one at the rear, the squatted, grasped the bottom edge, and lifted, grunting. There was a little thump as they shifted it for a better grip. Patrick held his breath, but the guard in front said, "Let's get this thing down. The queen must put stones in her clothing."

Sir James held the door open as they carried it out and maneuvered it down the winding stairs. His heart hammering with nerves, Patrick followed after them, the other man on his heels. The guard in front was grunting. "Take some of the weight, damn you."

"Be careful!" Patrick yelped. "Crichton will have your heads if you delay the queen's departure by breaking her kist."

Slowly they worked their load round and down the stairs and through the hall. The queen was talking to Crichton, telling him that the king needed a weapon master and that it was not right to expect to expect Sir Patrick to serve both as master of the guard and weapon master. Crichton listened noncommittally, shrugged, and said he would consider it. The carter hurried around and helped the men-at-arms lift the kist into the space they'd saved for it in the second cart.

Crichton scowled. "Where is the king?"

"I think he went up on the parapet to watch them depart." Patrick offered his arm to the queen and escorted her to her horse and knelt to offer her his hands as a stirrup to step into. When she was mounted, there was nothing to do but watch the party, surrounded by their own small group of men-at-arms, ride through the towering gatehouse arch. Guards with crossbows looked down at the passing cavalcade. Soon he could hear the grind of the cart wheels and clatter of hooves on the cobbles of the bumpy slope down Arthur's Mount.

Patrick wiped his sweaty hands on the front of his doublet. Now he must see that the king was not missed before there was time for the queen's party to reach Queensferry Crossing and cross the Forth on the awaiting ferry. He forced a chuckle. "There will be a good deal more peace and quiet now with the queen and her chattering daughters gone."

Crichton grunted. "Aye. Less chatter will be a relief." He turned and strode toward the gate of the inner bailey, Patrick following behind.

In the smaller hall of David's Tower, Crichton threw himself into the high-backed lord's chair and called for some wine. A manservant hurried out to do his bidding. A boy was tending the fire in the hearth and the men-at-arms had returned to their post but otherwise the place was unnervingly quiet. To break the silence, Patrick said, "I dinnae have that much to do yet as the king's master of guard. Tutoring him in weapons is nae burden. Though if you think another master would be better..." He shrugged.

Crichton waited until the servant returned with the flagon and handed him a goblet. The scent was tempted so Patrick poured some for himself. Crichton swirled the wine thoughtfully. "He's too young to need a weapon master. That can wait for a bit. Nae point in spending the money for it when you can do it as well. And you're right." He gave Patrick a sharp look. "You do nae have much to do."

"When the king is grown and no longer under your care, the matter will be different. But for the nonce, it does give me something to keep me out of trouble." He laughed. "And My Lord father one of these days will expect me to wed."

Crichton raised his eyebrows. "I hope you would nae be thinking of bringing her here to live. I'll nae pay your wife's keep."

Patrick drank deep from his goblet as he rolled his eyes. He sighed in satisfaction. At least the old king had laid in good wine, because he was sure Crichton would never have spent the gold for the malmsey that was so sweet on the tongue. "I had nae thought of it, but I have lands and a manor any bride would no doubt prefer to a grim pile like Edinburgh Castle, grand as it is."

Crichton's scowl deepened. "It is the strongest castle in Scotland, you whelp."

"Certes, it is, My Lord." Patrick held up and hand and smiled. "But strong castles are more suited to a fighting man such as you than to a young bride."

The chancellor eyed Patrick as though suspecting he was making a jape. Keeping his face blank, Patrick refilled his own goblet and offered more to Crichton.

"Where is his grace?" a voice called from the stairs. James's tutor came in. The priest was a small, dark man. His cassock was dark; his eyes were dark and quick. Fuzzy brown hair encircled his tonsure. "His grace has not come for his lesson. If he is in the practice yard, he must be sent to me."

Patrick smiled. "He cannot stand to be still. You ken how the lad is. I'll go find him for you." Careful to keep his movements leisurely, he finished his wine and left the cup on the table to stroll out into the sunlight. He supposed he had better pretend to actually search for the king to make it look good. He called to one of the men-at-arms standing guard near the gate to the lower bailey, "If you see the king, tell him his tutor is seeking him." The he chuckled. "Nae, instead send someone for me."

The guard grinned. "Aye, he is nae great one for his studies."

First, Patrick went to the practice yard where a dozen men-at-arms hacking at practice dummies all assured him they'd not seen the king. The stable master said the same. He climbed to the mews where a gray-haired cadger was whispering to a hawk as he fed it. The king's gyrfalcon was still on its perch, and the man said he'd not seen the king all day. By this time, Patrick felt almost alarmed and chuckled.

Back in the hall, Patrick suggested to the tutor that the king was out of sight, scrambling on the ramparts and towers as he was wont to do. The man shook his head. "Keeping him at his studies is more than I can do."

Crichton shrugged. "I always thought the late king was too learned. What needs a king with learning when he has clerics?"

Hours passed with no sign of the king. Patrick had almost convinced himself that the king was really missing, so he decided it was time to suggest that Crichton order a full search of the castle. There would be chaos when the king was not found. Patrick wondered how long it would take before word came from Stirling Castle that he was safely in the queen's hands. He huffed. It was time to face a doubtlessly furious keeper of the royal castle.

When Patrick re-entered the great hall, it took every ounce of his self-control to rush across the long room and face Crichton. It was quietly busy. A couple of merchants had come with some complaint about the behavior of castle guards; a trio of children played hide and seek behind the pillars in a distant corner; and half a dozen soldiers lounged on benches as they waited for the dinner hour.

"Have you found him?" Crichton said with studied calm.

"No, My Lord. You ken he is wild for adventure, so there is no telling what cranny or turret he has climbed to, but we must find him. I'll need help for the search."

"Of course." Crichton's tone indicated he didn't believe a word Patrick had said. "Because you do not have him hidden to be stolen away by the queen."

Patrick sighed heavily. "I am sure you had the queen watched as she boarded the ferry at the crossing. They must have seen that she truly left. I am nae scheming to take the lad anywhere. My only concern is his safety. Holy Jesu only kens where he may have gone. We must search for him."

"I ken that we must find him," Crichton said testily. He hated giving the impression he was not in control or that his power was slipping. He could not afford to be viewed as weak. "Someone must have sneaked him out of the castle. If not you, then who?"

"I have nae left the gates, Sir William, so it certainly was nae I. He can climb like a wiry mountain goat. I think he just found a place to slip over the wall. He hates that he's been confined and merely is hiding. Or worse, he tried to follow his mother's party and is wandering on the road."

"Odd," said Crichton. "Very odd that he should disappear so soon after they left."

"What's odd about a daring boy going off on his own? I'm surprised it has nae happened sooner."

"Mayhap is merely coincidence," Crichton said, steepling his beringed fingers. "He must be found and if he is not, I will find out who and how he was removed."

A chill went through Patrick, but he kept the same worried frown on his face. "If I fail in my duty to protect the king, my life won't be worth a groat. So I beg you, My Lord, let me take a dozen men. Let us search the castle more thoroughly. If he is nae found, we had best search the road to Queensferry in case he did try to follow his mother's cavalcade."

Crichton clutched the arms of his chair and leaned forward, jaws clinched so that the muscles stood out and his face turned red. "Get me that lad."

Patrick's chill deepened. "You may depend upon me, My Lord." He motioned around the great hall. "Should I take these men with me since they're at hand?"

"Go search every road and alley. I'll have the castle searched whilst you do that." Crichton paused and then said, "And my men shall ensure that you return to the castle rather than ... disappear after the lad."

"Naturally."

"Good. Then you understand me. Now dinnae just stand there. Start searching!"

There were still hours of daylight left. Patrick watched clouds that roiled above the distant Pentland Hills, catching the light like swirling surf. Nearer below him, shadows crept across the fields and into the city. Every inch of the castle and the road to the ferry crossing had been searched for the king. Now they had men-at-arms out searching the city and the nearby hills. No one dared approach Lord Crichton whose every word was a curse for the Queen who had to be to blame, he was sure.

Patrick had paced the parapet all day, until his legs were so weary they felt as heavy as logs. After three long days he still awaited word that James was safe. When he heard the rapid hoof beats of a horse galloping up the steep road to the gate he breathed a soft, "Deo gratias." He hurried to the square tower that guarded the gate as a horseman wearing royal livery pulled up his lathered horse, shouting, "Hoi, The gate! I bear a message for Lord Crichton."

Patrick raced down the steps to the bailey and into the hall. There was nothing to do but wait, so he called for wine and appropriated the lord's chair with its cushioned seat, stretched out his legs, and took a drink. He might as well relax and be comfortable until the coming storm hit.

The hall was restful in the quiet of the late afternoon. The mid-day dinner was cleared away, the fire crackled comfortably, there was the quiet sound of servants in the kitchen going about their late day business. A manservant came in to light the candles, bothering no one as he climbed a ladder to reach them high on the thick columns. The early evening was still and easy—for the nonce.

Soon there was an uproar in the inner bailey loud enough to be heard through the thick doors: Crichton's voice screaming, "Someone shall pay for this! Never doubt it." and the thump of heavy feet. Figures nothing more than silhouettes in the murk came through the door. A tall figure, scarecrow-like in spite of his billowing cloak, stamped to face Patrick.

Crichton's glared into Patrick's face, his mouth twisted into a snarl. "How did you get him out of the castle?" He waved a parchment at Patrick and then crumpled it in his fist.

Patrick shook his head, looking wide-eyed, although cold sweat trickled down his back. If Crichton decided to make Patrick pay for the king's escape, no one would stop him. In this castle, all the power was his and he could call down retribution like the hand of God. Patrick knew that whatever protection the king and his own father offered would not serve him now. His only protection was to convince Crichton of his ignorance. He feigned an offended look and said,

"Whatever their plots, they did nae trust me with them, My Lord."

Crichton continued to stare at Patrick, breathing fast as though he'd been running. His face was mottled red with rage, and his face twisted into a grimace. "I care nothing except for the king's safety. Nothing!"

This was no time to call Crichton a liar, so Patrick said, "Of course, My Lord. And where could the king be safer than here under your protection?"

"You had to have knowledge of this." Crichton's face was twisted with rage.

"I swear I do not. By all the saints, I swear it. I dinnae ken where the king is." He motioned to the message Crichton had crumped and thrown on the floor. "You have news of him there? He is safe?"

Crichton stared at him as though he were an idiot. "Did I nae say that? And I welcomed her most gladly. There was nae reason to steal him from my care." The red was fading from his face and his voice was quieter.

Patrick swallowed a snort at Crichton's lie. "The queen seems rash and thoughtless at times, but that is the way with women. And I think mayhap Sir James Stewart encourages her in it." He jumped up. "Forgive me, My Lord. Take your seat and let me pour you some wine."

He turned his back on the man to pour fill the goblet, to hide that his hands were shaking. "Where did they take the lad then?" he asked.

"Stirling! To that cur, Callendar!"

Patrick took a deep breath before he turned to hand Crichton a filled goblet. "You mean they intend to remain at Stirling?"

A muscle in Crichton's cheek twitched. He was breathing hard. "Are you a dolt? Of course, they are staying in Stirling. There is no way Callendar will let the king go!"

Patrick scowled, crossing his arms. "Why did they keep me in the dark? I am supposed to be master of the king's guard! And what am I supposed to do here? You have no use for me."

Crichton mouth twisted into a snarl. "Blockhead." He threw his goblet at Patrick. Patrick jumped back as it clattered on the floor at his feet, wine spattered across his chest. "Get out of my sight. I have important things to consider. "

Patrick bowed deeply. He hurried to the door and into the upper bailey. Thankfully, he spotted Alex Boyd, sweaty from the practice yard, just emerging from the gate. Patrick frantically motioned to him. When Boyd reached him, he threw his arm around his friends shoulder and said, "There's news."

Alex Boyd raised his eyebrows, but Patrick shook his head, chewing his nether lip. He'd sooner not be seen by Crichton in case the man changed his mind and decided to hold him here. But he couldn't leave as he was. "Come." He spun on his heel and hurried into the hall. Crichton had turned his back and was staring glumly in the low flames in the hearth. With a deep breath, Patrick strolled quietly past and began to climb the winding stairs but they once they were out of sight of the hall, he ran.

When Patrick's chamber door slammed behind them, he tore off his cloak and began unbuttoning his wine-soaked doublet. "The king is with the queen at Stirling Castle. Crichton just received word."

"Och, that explains all the whispering amongst the men in the practice yard." Boyd squinted suspiciously to study Patrick. "You kent where he was all this time."

Patrick tossed aside his doublet and tore off his shirt. "I learnt where he was only today." He shrugged at Alex Boyd's incredulous snort.

"You did nae trust me with the secret!"

"All right. Yes, I kent where he was. I was sworn to

secrecy. You would have kept such an oath as well." He hurried to the kist in a corner where he armor was stored, and pulled out the thick, padded arming doublet that would protect his skin from the heavy plate. "Help me with this. Crichton telt me to get out of his sight, and I must be gone before he changes his mind." He turned to Alex Boyd. "You need to come with me."

Boyd crossed his arms over his chest, glowering at Patrick. "Why should I if I am nae trusted."

"Damn it, man, it was nae my secret to tell." He laced the front of the thick, padded doublet and drew on his woolen chausses that would protect his legs. "Forbye, do you want to wait to try to convince Crichton that you did nae ken? Now help me buckle on this cuirass. We cannot chance riding all the way to Stirling just the two of us unarmored."

Patrick was twitching with impatience as Alex Boyd buckled the metal pieces into place. At last he buckled his sword belt around his waist, sheathed his dirk on the other side and picked up his helm. He grabbed up his heaviest, fur lined cloak and hurried after Alex to his chamber to do the same for him.

Alex peered suspiciously down the stairs as the went. "We can sneak out, I think. Most likely Crichton has left the hall."

Patrick had to laugh. If there was one thing you didn't do in armor was sneak. "Nae point in trying to sneak. We walk out like the knights we are, going about our business. If any question us, we are doing what Lord Crichton said to do."

Brave words, but when he peered around the corner, he was relieved to see that Crichton was not there, and he shook his head at his nerves. He straightened his back and strode across the hall and into the bailey, helm tucked beneath his arm. So far their plan had gone alarmingly well. In his experience, plans rarely went off without something going wrong. But he and Alex strolled to the stable and saddled their horses. A stable boy glanced at them but went about his business raking soiled straw.

Patrick hung his helm by its strap, put his shield on his back and mounted. They rode side by side at a slow walk across the yard and into the portcullis gate. Never had the shadows of the passage seemed so dark or the murder holes so large, but in a minute they were through. His shoulders twitched, expecting a crossbow bolt as his horse clattered down the steep road. But for once, a plan did work. Just to be sure Crichton did not send someone after them, they'd not take the Queensferry Crossing. The way to the bridge would be longer, but Patrick was taking no chances.

"I still feel their eyes on my back," Boyd muttered.

"Aye, but no arrows." Suddenly Patrick was laughing. Perhaps he was not so bad a spy after all.

8

Patrick rode slowly up Stirling town's thronged High Street with Alex Boyd close behind. Both horses were too done to do more than skitter at rowdy shouts from vendors and the bangs as stalls were disassembled. He looked about hoping to see someone he knew and learn what was happening at the castle since the king had been taken there.

"We could just go straight to the castle," Boyd said.

"It may come to that," said Patrick. "But I'd like to ken what is happening first, at least to be sure the king is there. And there is one who can tell us, indeed." He spotted Sir William Stewart, the Black Knight's brother, walking out of a tavern door. "Sir William!"

The knight halted mid-stride to shade his eyes with a hand and scan the crowd for who had called out to him. A bustling serving girl carrying a basket piled with kale and beans collided with him, beans scattering across the cobbles. Glowering, she flounced around him.

"Sir Patrick," the man exclaimed, ignoring the woman's

ire. "We were concerned that you might have trouble persuading Crichton to allow you to leave. The king has been asking every hour or so when you would arrive." He grinned.

Patrick dismounted and stretched his aching shoulders after such a long ride with only stops to briefly rest the horses. "Then the king is still at Stirling Castle?"

"Och, everyone is at the castle." He waved an arm in the general direction of the crag of Castle Hill. A laborer dodged and cursed at him as a fool of a duniwassal. "Come along. The king will be overjoyed and the queen glad to nae have to answer his questions on when he'll have another lesson with his sword."

"Then I'll join them right away. How did Callendar receive them?"

"He was glad to receive the king at least." He gave an acid smile. "I was seeking more congenial company, but I am headed there now." Sir William shouted at a servant who led his horse over. He mounted and turned its head to ride up the hill.

Patrick stretched his neck, grimaced at Boyd, mounted and followed up the steep slope to the fortress that towered atop the rocky crag.

Following Sir William through rooms fusty with the scent of musk and lavender and smoke from oak fires in the hearths, Patrick was surprised to see more familiar faces than had ever appeared at Edinburgh Castle, men who had ridden with them after Stewart and more who had visited his father's lands for hunting and politicking. Men he hadn't seen in a long while were sitting about playing cards and throwing dice.

"I recognize you," a voice said from beside him. "You're Lord Gray's son." He turned to find the fat, gray haired Earl of Avondale at his elbow. His girth and age had not kept him from wearing a houppelande of shimmering blue brocade.

"What brings you to Stirling, clanking in armor and covered in dirt?" He smiled sourly, which set his jowls aquiver.

"Lord Avondale," Patrick said formally, looking into that sweat-slick face level with his. "I am rejoining the king's household. As for my appearance, I have only just arrived and have nae had time to remove my armor."

"Ah, well." The nobleman gave him a searching look. "Your sire is here as well. He seems pleased with the king's change in residence."

"Is he? His grace had grown restless at Edinburgh, so the change may be a good thing."

"So you will continue as a gentleman of the king's bedchamber." He turned back the wide sleeves of his gown so that the cherry-colored silk lining showed. "That will be a peaceful position in a child's household. No worry about whether you have any skill in the field. My sons have been in France for jousting."

"For the king's sake, I would hope it is peaceful."

"Gray," Sir William said, "come. You will want to pay your respects to her grace."

"A pity to have nae chance for gaining renown," Avondale said. With considerable relief, Patrick bowed to him before turning to follow William Stewart from the room.

The innermost chamber was crowded with courtiers and servants. Annabella smiled, and he bowed to her from across the room. Near an arched window a table was set up with a flagon and wine goblets and a large stand of candles. On one side, Queen Joan, smiling with a look almost of restored youth, her blue eyes and fair beauty set off with blue velvet and green silk, was talking with a tall man with a short black beard whom he recognized from that day at the coronation, Sir Alexander Callendar, Lord of Callendar. On this side of the table sat the Black Knight of Lorne, Sir James Stewart, clad in his usual black silk and broad hands folded on the table in front of him. He laughed at something the queen said.

Sir William slapped his brother on the shoulder to get his attention. The conversation paused and Patrick kissed the queen's hand while Alex bowed, hanging back. A servant thrust a stool behind him at the queen's command and Patrick found himself seated and commanded to give an account of how Lord Crichton had received the news of the king's presence in Lord Callendar's care. Callendar watched him impassively as Patrick recounted Crichton's rage. Sir James signaled a servant and whispered a command, but the queen listened, watching closely and looking amused as he described their hasty flight from Edinburgh.

"So he gave no idea of taking any action in retaliation?" Callendar asked.

"He was angry enough, but what can he do?"

"Aye," said Callendar thoughtfully, "No saying, is there? How many men does he have readily to hand would you say?"

"About the number you would expect in a castle as large as Edinburgh," Patrick said. He wrinkled his brow as he calculated. "Mayhap seven hundred. Certainly under a thousand, but of course more on his own lands."

"About what I estimated..." Said Sir James. "Certainly not enough to seize the king from us here."

"Hmmm..." The queen stared at Patrick, candlelight shimmering on silk and jewels. "So it is most vital to keep the king contented to be surrounded by guards yet again. He will be more than pleased to see you, Sir Patrick. And you as well, Sir Alexander. But for now I know you both will want to be free of the dust of the road."

Patrick took that as a dismissal. The servant Sir James had whispered to bowed to Patrick and begged him to follow to a chamber set aside for them. But Patrick held up his hand when his father, across the room locked gazes with him. After nodding, his lord father said for him to remove the travel soil and meet him in the garden courtyard. The servant led him and Alex through the crowded rooms and up a winding stair into a bedroom chamber, where warm water for washing and their saddle bags already awaited them.

Patrick groaned with relief as Boyd helped him shed his armor. Then he did the same for the other man. He shook out the doublet and chausses from his saddle bags and wondered how long it would take for him to manage to have more clothes sent from home. Again. He suspected that Crichton would be in no hurry to send what he had abandoned at Edinburgh Castle.

Boyd threw himself down on the bed. "Thank the blessed saints my father is nae here, and I don't have to go scurrying off to report to him."

"Aye, the bed is where I would rather be as well." It was a wide one with a deep feather mattress that would be no hardship to share. With each of their armor piled in a corner to await cleaning, Patrick looked around the simple chamber. "Stirling is more crowded than I expected, but this will do well enough." They wouldn't be the only knights sharing a chamber.

Boyd muttered his agreement. By the time Patrick closed the door, he was loudly snoring. Patrick had never before been in Stirling Castle, but once he found a servant, the man pointed the way to the courtyard. By the time Patrick stepped into it, his father was outside awaiting him. High windows glowed and the sky was purple, stars strewn across like diamonds tossed upon velvet.

Lord Gray stopped in the center of the courtyard, and thoughtfully stroked his mustache. "Go over again what Crichton said when he learnt the king was gone and when the message arrived."

"The one thing I am certain of is that he was furious,"

Patrick said. "We searched for two days but long before we stopped the search he had guessed that the queen has stolen away the lad. At first, he accused me of conspiring to steal the king from him, but he could nae dispute that I was still thon. I convinced him I was too stupid to be trusted with such a secret." Patrick's mouth twisted in a wry smile. He suspected that his father and Kennedy did think he was stupid, but used him anyway. "When the message arrived from Stirling, I've never seen him in such a rage. I expected to be thrown in the dungeon. I'm certain had we stayed, that is where we would be."

Lord Gray was still stroking his mustache when he said, "That does nae matter." Patrick's laugh must have sounded bitter, because it earned him a sharp look. "Dinnae be a dunce, Patrick. That is nae what I mean. There is more going on than you ken. I have less influence with the queen than I hoped, and with Kennedy on his way to Florence..." He shook his head.

Patrick glanced around to be sure that no one else was in the courtyard. In the dark, he could not make out his father's features, only the gleam of his eyes. "Less influence? About what?"

"You must have seen her fondness for Sir James."

"Aye." Patrick cocked his head as he thought back over when he seen them together. "There is nae missing that. But he is a renowned knight as well as bonnie and well-found. Is that so strange?"

"Aye, but she is the queen." Lord Gray lowered his voice so that Patrick had to step closer to hear. "He is one of the Douglas alliance, and Callendar has nae forgiven the Douglases for supporting Crichton to be chancellor." Lord Gray sighed and threw back his head to stare up at the stars. "And I believe that the queen means to marry him."

"Wait." Patrick shook his head. "That makes nae sense.

Sir James helped sneak the king out of Crichton's hands. He helped bring him to Callendar for safe keeping. Surely that makes up for any offense from the Black Douglas naming Crichton the chancellor."

"It may make up for an insult, but Callendar won't trust him. Or the queen after they're wed." Lord Gray clasped Patrick's shoulder hard. "She must be warned that if she marries Sir James that Callendar will consider it a threat to possessing the king. It will be a threat he cannot, will not ignore."

Patrick rubbed his hand down his face hard. Between the castle towers, the moon hung behind thin, blowing clouds, looking old and tarnished. "The king will nae be a child forever. They are earning more hatred than I can even tell you. The day will come when he will have power."

"That may be. But that day is years in the future. For now, Callendar is as dangerous as Crichton." He paused for a moment. "I think more dangerous than Crichton, and I dinnae ken what he will do if I cannot convince the queen to delay marrying Sir James. If she would wait, mayhap until Kennedy returns... Kennedy is diplomat enough that he might smooth matters over. The result of their marrying now will be beyond my power to control."

"I dinnae ken what I can do about it, My Lord. The queen is unlikely to listen to me. Nor is the Black Knight."

"Play the same game here that you did at Edinburgh. Try to gain Callendar's trust. See what you can learn of his plans. If my fears are correct, it may be that if you have his trust, you will be the best person to mediate."

Patrick tugged on the tuft of the narrow beard on his chin. "What do you think he will do?"

"They have put themselves at his mercy, bringing the lad here. What's done is done. I cannot guess what he will do, but the queen is putting herself in danger. Of that I am sure."

Patrick stared down at his feet as he tried to untangle the threads of politics. "The Black Douglas supported Crichton," he said slowly.

"And is dead."

"So the queen decided she could safely remove the king from Crichton." He shook his head. "So why now marry an ally of the dead earl? That makes no sense."

Lord Gray grunted in disgust. "Can you expect a woman, even a de Beaufort, to make a sensible decision? As you said, he is a braw man, well-found as well. She likes him, and she trusts him."

"But you think he cannot protect her?"

"No. Not against Callendar. The question is what will Callendar do to protect his power base?"

"Mayhap. The queen, I think, may be a sharper woman than you believe. But be that as it may, My Lord, do you seriously expect me to gain close to Callendar? He will think me someone of no power or importance. Which is the truth."

"You helped gain the king away from Crichton. That he is aware of. Ask him if there is aught you can do to ensure that king's safety. Say that you fear that Crichton may try to regain him and offer to ensure that cannot happen. You are master of the king's guard. Use that." His father thumped Patrick on the chest with his forefinger. "Use your brain. I hope that you have one."

"I am better with fighting than with words." He stared at his lord father silently and then said, "I will never be a diplomat however much that disappoints you."

"Well, do this. You must."

"Aye, My Lord." He frowned, but there was no point in arguing. "I shall speak to Callendar."

"And Patrick..." His father crossed his arms, looking him up and down like a prize bull he was considering purchasing.

"We need all the allies we can manage, so I have decided to begin negotiations for your marriage."

"What?"

"It is past time. It is almost two years since Margaret died. You're mourned long enough. And we need this."

"Who?" Damn them all. They had him dance like a puppet on a string, and the pain of Margaret dying trying to bear him a child was a grief that still haunted his sleep. Besides, if he were to marry again, he had a right to make his own choice.

"Lord Forbes was close to the Earl of Angus, married to his sister." The Earl of Angus had recently died leaving a twelve year old son as his heir, so Forbes might well be looking for new allies, Patrick considered. His father went on, "They have a daughter of marriageable age who would be a good match. Since she serves the queen, she could be useful in persuading the queen to act... sensibly."

"You mean Annabella Forbes? Does she ken about this proposed match?"

"Of course not. Do you have some objection to her? Is there something wrong with her?"

"She is a pleasant lass." Patrick blinked several times. "Brave, I think, and loyal to the queen." He blushed, thankful his father couldn't see it in the dark. "I like her."

His father shrugged, not much interested in whether he like her or not, turned on his heel, and walked away. A rectangle of light broke the darkness and he was silhouetted in the doorway. The door closed, leaving Patrick alone. He looked up at the night sky, breathed in the crisp night air. He blew out a breath.

Damn them for the manipulating bastards they were. But purely by accident, Annabella would be...a good choice. He shook his head. He could live with that, would be pleased with it. He would have to hope she felt the same. Perhaps it would be a good idea to talk to her about it.

Exhaustion swept over him like an engulfing tide. He scratched at the heavy scruff on his face. He needed nothing more than a bath and a good night's sleep. Tomorrow when he was clean and rested, all of this might make sense, so he could deal with it.

❧ 9 ❧

The next morning, Patrick brushed most of the wrinkles out of his doublet, donned it, and went looking for Callendar. He wandered through the halls, asked several servants if they knew where the man might be found, and managed to lose himself twice in the maze like fortress, but at last a guard pointed him toward a windowless closet that Callendar was using as a privy chamber.

Patrick's knock brought a curt voice asking who it was. When he answered, Callendar replied to enter.

Two men stood in the small chamber. In the middle, a table took up most of the space with a large map spread out beside a stand of newly lit candles. On the far side, Sir Alexander Callendar, Lord Callendar and Keeper of Stirling Castle, a wiry, fair-haired man in blue-colored velvet, was speaking to a cleric, clean-shaven and tonsured in dark brocade, plump, beringed hands resting on the table as he studied the map.

Sir Alexander looked closely at Patrick with round, pale eyes and then cast a pointed glance at the man beside him.

"My lord bishop, here is someone who can answer questions for us." Patrick realized that this was John Cameron, Bishop of Glasgow, former Chancellor of Scotland and still Keeper of the Privy Seal. Patrick found himself kneeling to kiss the ring of the most powerful man of the former king's reign.

"Sir Patrick." Cameron gave Patrick the practiced smile of a statesman. "I understand you feel that Crichton does not have the men to attack Stirling?"

"No, sir. Not at Edinburgh, but if he called upon the men in his own lands..." Patrick frowned thoughtfully. "And he has been in close communion with the Earl of Avondale. I dinnae ken how many spears Avondale could raise if he took Crichton's part."

"He will nae chance attacking Stirling whilst we hold the king here," Cameron said. "Not and give the appearance of attacking the person of the king. It would be lèse-majesté or so we would name it."

Patrick stepped closer to the map and looked down at it as though it would answer the questions that swirled in his mind. "But he is chancellor and holds the great seal. Could that give him the right to call upon aid in recovering the king?" For an army that could not easily cross the Firth of Forth, it would be several days travel from Edinburgh to Stirling.

"He cannot call a parliament without the presence of the king. That pulls his teeth. Moreover, any call for raising an army, I can meet with a proclamation signed by the king himself over his privy seal. The queen was given the right to possession of the king after the last parliament, so she has every right to have him sign such a document."

"How well do acquainted are you with Crichton, sir?" Patrick chewed on his lower lip for a moment. "He is a wrathful and determined man. I cannae believe he will simply accept losing possession of the king. I saw the rage he was in when he realized the queen had him."

Callendar shook his head. "The matter of the queen—"

Cameron brusquely cut him off. "She did well to bring the king to you. Now we must concentrate on keeping him in our hands."

Callendar grunted softly. "Borthwell Castle is near Crichton's lands. Sir William Borthwell is on good terms with Crichton—at my behest. I'll see that he apprises us if Crichton raises his spears."

"He is more likely to copy the queen's methods and try to regain the king by stealth." He stared at Patrick for a moment, candle light flickering on broad brow and rounded cheeks. "That is what we must guard against. He must be closely guarded at all times. That will be your task. Keep the lad busy and safe. He is eager for more lessons with the sword I am told."

Callendar grunted in agreement. "My son will join him in these lessons. The king is given to enjoying too much low company of the stable boys and ghillies that he should be weaned from. I sent to the training yard where you'll find them."

The bishop held out his hand, so Patrick went down on one knee to kiss his episcopal ring. Cameron made the sign of the cross over him and gave him his blessing. Then he said, "If you learn anything that would affect the king's person, I charge you to report it to me."

"Gladly, My Lord." Patrick said as though he truly intended to spy for yet another faction.

Young James and David Callendar were nowhere to be found in the training yard. Shrieks from outside the gate let Patrick in that direction. He chucked as he watched James lead the way as several rough clad lads followed him sliding down the muddy slope of Castle Hill on their rears, at play in a game of hurlyhacket. He sent their playmates to find other fun and took the king and his companion in his charge for work with the sword and then with their bows.

That evening when King James was abed, Patrick went looking for Annabella. He found her near the Princesses bed chambers and proposed a walk to discuss the last few days' doings. In the haze of near dusk, they strolled to the high summit of the castle rock, where the craggy edge plummeted with a sheer drop to the plain of Forth. Summer light lasted late into the night, so only a few stars were winking out in the purple tinted sky.

They found a stone outcrop to sit on and she settled with a deep sigh, tilting back her head. "It is nice to breathe the fresh air of the outside."

Patrick sat beside her, his thigh just brushing the edge of her skirts. He pointed south. "Look." He pointed to a cross shape of stars barely visible in the still darkening sky. "You can see the Summer Triangle."

Annabella leaned forward to follow where he pointed. "So you can." There was a smile in her voice. Turning her head, she pointed further north. "And there is the handle of the Plough. But it is nae dark enough yet to see the North Star."

He made a sort of grunt in agreement and propped his elbows on his thighs. He hadn't quite decided how to talk about all that he had on his mind. After a deep breath, he blurted, "The queen quite likes the Sir James Stewart?"

"Aye." Annabella's voice still held the sound of a smile. "She does."

When Patrick turned to look in her face, he could barely see in the fading light that she was indeed smiling. "I fear that they may decide to marry."

She wrinkled her brow. "Why is that a fear? He is a braw knight, and surely after all that happened, she has a right to a some happiness."

"The king is only two years dead. You dinnae think it is soon?"

"Two years is long enough to mourn. A decent period." She looked at him closely, quiet for a long moment. "What is it that you are truly saying?"

Patrick ran his hand over his cheeks, freshly shaven for her. The last thing he wanted was to offend her. "I do fear it. But you have the right of it. That's nae the reason." He turned and took one of her hands. "I fear how Alexander Callendar will react. She still has the custody of the king, officially at least. But he controls him and means to continue to doing so."

She shook her head. "That has nothing to do with the queen marrying. She wants Sir Alexander to keep young James from the hands of Crichton. She needs him. Why should change that?"

"That is nae how Callendar will see it. Stewart is allied with the Douglases." He blew out a breath. "Aye, the head of the Black Douglases is dead. Angus favored Callendar but with him dead, there is a vacuum of power that cannae continue. I fear..." He paused, frowning in thought. "I very much fear that if she marries James Stewart that Callendar will act against them."

"But how? What can he do?"

"I'm nae sure what way that blow will fall, but it will be a harsh one." He ran his thumb over the softness of her hand, liking the velvety feel of it. "He is the keeper of Stirling Castle and has all of us in the palm of his hand. Certes, Crichton would nae come to her aid and Sir James has at most a small force at his call unless Angus defended him. Would he declare war with the man who holds the king? I dinnae think he will do so."

She seemed not at all to mind his caress of her hand and in fact curled her fingers around his. "Sir Patrick, she is set on this marriage. She cares very much for Sir James. He has stood by her in all of her trials as no one else has. I swear to you, he's a good man."

"Good man or nae, it is dangerous. Can you persuade her just to wait? I dinnae say she should change her mind, but put the marriage off for a time. Mayhap when Bishop Kennedy returns? I am sure he would take her part."

"She will nae wait that long. Who knows how long he may be detained with the Pope? She means to marry, and she trusts Callendar. His wife is one of us, a lady-in-waiting. The friendship is long."

"Will you at least mention to her that Callendar may be wroth at such a marriage? Give her a warning?"

She pulled her hand out of his. While they talked, it had grown dark and he could no longer make out her expression but she sounded annoyed when she said, "I could ask her how she thinks he will feel about it. But she wants a man to cherish her."

"Surely other women want that as well." He reached to take back her hand and turned to face her. He could smell the rose scent that she wore as it wafted on the night air. "I dinnae mean that I am against marriage, My Lady. I—" He broke off when she slapped her other hand over her mouth to suppress a giggle. Now it was he who dropped her hand. He jerked back. "Are you laughing at me?"

She retrieved his hand in both of hers. "I promise that I am not. I dinnae ken why I laughed." She leaned forward and kissed his cheek then she whispered, "I am nae against marriage—"

There was still just a trace of laughter in her voice but he did not mind, so took the opportunity to put his arm around her to keep her close. She leaned into his embrace and leaned against him. She encircled him with her arms, pulled him to her, and the rest of her words were lost against his mouth. He kissed her gently at first, but it wasn't enough. She knotted her fists in his double, grasping him harder against her. He groaned, low in his throat, and bent back her head across his arm and kissed her hard, with an intensity that made her cling to him. Then they overbalanced, rolled over the edge outcrop and onto the grass, tangled together, still kissing as they laughed. They laughed until they gasped with breathlessness. She untangled from him and stood, brushing bits of grass from her skirt. He jumped up and brushed her back where she could not reach. If she minded when he ran his hand down her hips, she did not say.

"Your father is here," Patrick said, as he brushed away a bit more imaginary grass. |"Tomorrow, I shall speak to him." Be damned if he would have his father continue to run his life. It was time time... no, it was past time to take more of his life into his own hands. He'd not leave the matter to his lord father. He would put behind him his grief.

They did not speak as hand-in-hand they made for the royal quarters. Patrick knew that the world had changed for him. The future could hardly be more uncertain, but he had gained something precious. A woman he treasured to share and build that future as best they could. With one last kiss at her door, he went to a sleepless bed where the myriad possibilities and problems of that future twisting and twining in his head.

10

Patrick motioned for Alexander Forbes, a sinewy old man with a thin mouth under a thin beard, to join him in a quiet corner. Early in the day only a couple of men sat across the room playing dice and talking about hunting. He gulped a bit when Forbes gave him a cool look. Bringing marriage up seemed harder than he had expected. "Your daughter..." He cleared his throat. "I would like her hand in marriage if you would consider it."

"I've discussed a marriage contract with your lord father."

"He mentioned as much to me, but a man grown can discuss his own marriage. You already ken that my father has no objection." He tapped his cheek, trying to hide his nervousness. "I have certain lands obtained of my father lands in Kinneff with two good farms and a strong manor house. I'll provide for her well."

Forbes narrows his eyes. "Are you saying I'll nae give my lass a good dower that you must provide for her."

"Heaven forfend, no, My Lord. But her dower will be hers for if ever she had need of it." He patted the air as though to soothe the insulted man. "Since you and my father see no objection to the match, we could agree and settle on a date for a betrothal, I hope."

Forbes blew out a scornful puff through his lips. "You young are always so impatient."

Patrick threw a glance towards the two men dicing who seemed to be paying them no mind. He lowered his voice to say, "My lord, with the state of the realm, is it nae better to have matters settled as much as we can? She and I are both closely tied to the royal family. Our marriage will only strengthen our hand." If that was not the real reason he wanted to marry Annabella, their fathers had no need to know of it. "Is there aught to be gained from delaying?"

Forbes worked his mouth for a moment as he considered Patrick's words. "Mayhap not. If it is to be done, it is well done soon, I suppose. Have you talked to your father about this?"

"He told me last eve that he favored the match, but we talked no more than that. You had already discussed the contract so it should be a simple matter." Since the man seemed to be reasonable, Patrick's face brightened with a smile. "A betrothal will take our minds off so much worry the past few days."

The slap Forbes gave him on the shoulder was harder than expected from his wiry frame. "I shall speak to your sire. I think we can quickly agree. Once the betrothal is held, we'll have the banns cried. Mayhap you won't be so bad a husband for my lass." He gave Patrick a hard look. "You'd better not be."

"The best that I ken how to be, My Lord. I give you my word on it."

It took a servant only a short time to locate Lord Gray and for him to join them. He looked less than pleased that Patrick had taken matters into his own hands, but since he wanted the match as well, he did no more than give Patrick a disapproving look before they sat and quickly agreed that he would receive as her dowry some land in Kincardine. A cleric would draw up the contract to be signed at the betrothal celebration.

❧ 11 ❧

It was the queen who took charge, beaming as she imposed her will on the celebration. Fresh rushes well mixed with lavender were strewn over the floor of the great hall. The cooks and kitcheners were exhorted to exert themselves to cope with the short notice. The whitest linen the royal castle had to offer was laid out on long trestle tables, commands were sent into Stirling Town to find dancers, mummers, and strolling players in addition to the one jester and the bard already in residence. James eagerly told his mother about a juggler who'd had a dog that jumped through hoops who been in the castle a few days before entertaining the children, so someone was sent to search for him as well.

While the queen kept the castle abustle in preparation for the celebration, his father, already resplendent in a red wool doublet, found Patrick glumly sponging his second doublet. Together they looked at the garment which was well-worn with the color beginning to fade in a few spots. As much as he could, Patrick preferred to dress in a practical manner, had never thought himself a popinjay, but there were some times when making an appearance was important. He did not want to humiliate either his bride-to-be or his family.

"This will nae do," his father said. "If you'd been less impatient, you could have had clothes sent from Kinneff."

Patrick sighed. "There must be a solution. Someone must be about my size from whom I could borrow something suitable."

Lord Gray looked him up and down as though he did not even know own his son's appearance. At last he said, "The Black Knight is about your height, although he's broader."

Lord Gray sent a castle servant bustling with a note for the Black Knight requesting the loan of something appropriate to the occasion. The knight appeared at the door, trailed by the servant who was loaded with a pile of clothing. "My new white doublet will do well. Since I've nae yet worn it, I'll make it a wedding gift," the man said with a grin. "There are blue chauses that should fit once they are pointed and gartered. And I brought a blue samite half cloak I fasten with a silver brooch. You'll look lordly enough to satisfy your bride, I give you my word."

Patrick swallowed a laugh. The Black Knight was well-founded indeed, but today he was right glad of it. But the Black Knight was correct. Tying the chauses tightly to his braes and fastening them with a garter made them show off the turn of his leg. The silky white doublet looked lordly enough over them with the cloak atop all.

The two men supervised his dressing with critical eyes but finally gave him a nod of approval. Patrick slapped the Black Knight's shoulder. He liked the man even if he thought wedding the queen would be a terrible error in judgement. "Thank you, sir. The last thing I would want to do is humiliate my bride or her father."

Lord Gray grunted. "Or me."

Patrick gave his father a bow. "Or you, sir." While they'd

taken so long preparing Patrick for the occasion, the sound of a harp mixed with the trill of pipes from the great hall. A singer's voice was muffled by the thick floors. In the great hall, torches shimmered against hammered silver, filling the hall with silvery light.

The air was filled with bright chatter from guests who were greeting each other and laughing beneath the sounds of the music. Yet Patrick could see dark suspicion in the pale eyes of Alexander Callendar, Lord Callendar, who already sat at the high table, He could see it in the eyes of Bishop Cameron between the soft folds of fat in his round face. But the queen was flushed and her eyes bright as she led Annabella to meet her father at the foot of the dais and Patrick caught his breath.

His bride was exquisite. She wore a deep blue gown of velvet that brought out the color of her eyes. Her tawny hair tumbled in waves across her bare shoulders and down to her waist. He saw no one else as he joined her to climb the two steps onto the dais and stand before the table where the marriage contract was laid out beside ink, quills and wax for the seals. Her father signed as did Patrick and his father. They all applied their seals and it was done. No one could gainsay the sweet kiss he claimed from her. Her blush to cheers and applause from the onlookers was only the sweeter.

He led her to take their place of honor next to Callendar and the queen. From a side table for the clergy, Bishop Cameron intoned a lengthy blessing. Annabella nudged him to cross himself at the end, for he was too lost in a daze to notice. The queen had harried the kitchen into serving a tasty banquet, even Patrick noticed. They started with crab and onion pie, duck roasted in honey, and then came beans savory with bacon, trout cooked in butter and goose stuffed with apples and oysters. Patrick made sure that Annabella had the choicest morsel of every dish set before them. By the time a sweet potage of ground almonds and candied ginger was served, Patrick was stuffed from the many courses but entertainment went on well into the night. Patrick did not mind since it gave him the chance to hold Annabella's hand and steal several kisses while the crowd cheered on the juggler and mummers who put on a loud performance.

12

AUGUST 3, 1439

The queen vigorously shook her head. "I agreed to wait until the two of you wed so as not to steal the attention from Annabella, but after you are one, I shall wed Sir James."

Annabella had warned him that it was hopeless, but Patrick had to try. "Your Grace, even waiting until Bishop Kennedy returns would nae be so long. You will need an ally if Callendar takes your wedding as a threat to his power." He propped his elbows on the table between them where they'd tossed aside their playing cards and leaned closer, making sure his voice was low. He did not want this conversation overheard by Callendar's wife who was at her embroidery on the other side of the solar. "The Black Knight is a braw man. I dinnae deny he'll be a good husband to you, but he has never been a friend to Callendar and that is not a man to ever forget or forgive a slight."

"Nonsense. I am on excellent terms with Sir Alexander. I would hardly have put my son in his care if I had not fully trusted him. He knows that."

Patrick sighed. They were out of time to convince her. In

a few moments, they would leave for the church for his wedding to Annabella, and all of his pleas had been for naught. That she had entrusted her son to Livingston, she was obviously convinced, would be enough. But every day Patrick saw Callendar and Cameron's greed for power grow. He was the queen's old friend an ally. She simply did not see it.

Patrick shook his head. There was nothing more he could do.

The queen smiled in forgiveness. "I know that you worry, but all will be well. Now you need to think of your bride."

With that he could agree so he returned her smile, glad that at least she wasn't angry at his appeals perhaps stated a bit too often. The Black Knight threw open the door and called, "It is time." They all rose, Patrick bowed to the queen as he was to enter through the side door of the Royal Chapel.

The Black Knight accompanied him, commenting as they went that the doublet he'd gifted Patrick with looked particularly well for the wedding. The priest, already in a lavishly embroidered alb, met them at the side door and to a small room where he told them to wait. He assured Patrick he would summon him at the right moment.

Through the closed door they heard the king chattering and the sounds of footsteps as the guests entered the chapel. Presently an altar boy opened the door and led them into the chapel. There they found the king, queen and princesses along with Lord Gray and Alex Boyd sitting on pews that had been moved into the chapel, awaiting the ceremony.

They all beamed as the two of them strode to the steps of the chancel where the priest awaited with a couple of acolytes. He turned to bow to the altar and then turned to face the congregation. When he raised his arms, from the front of the chapel, Annabella entered on her father's arm. They came to stand between Patrick and the Black Knight,

Forbes giving Patrick a solemn nod, but Patrick couldn't return it. His gaze was fixed on his bride.

She was stunning. A blush tinted her cheeks and her eyes gleamed. Dressed in rose colored silk trimmed with marten, her bodice was fitted and her long dagged sleeves almost reached the floor. A snood that sparkled with gems confined her hair. When she looked past her father, who stood between them, her gaze fixed on his.

When the priest asked who gave the woman to this man, Patrick started, having gotten lost in her eyes. Lord Forbes said, "I do."

Forbes gave her hand to Patrick, stepping away and Patrick's heart beat so hard he thought its thundering might be heard, but Annabella just smiled up at him. With a flourish, the Black Knight produced the ring for the priest to bless, a gift of the queen from her own jewelry. Patrick slipped it onto her finger, never letting her hand go. Then the priest declared them man and wife. She was his. That thought got him through the moments as they knelt for the priest's blessing.

Patrick found himself, not quite sure how it was all over, walking arm and arm through their guests to the door. The king skipped alongside them wondering loudly if he would marry someday, but declaring it a pretty boring business. The princesses were all chattering except the *Muta Domina* who was signing excitedly and one of her sisters signing back.

He would have liked to take his bride to his own house at Kinneff but that was near Aberdeen and impossible. Instead there was the wedding feast to get through. The banquet far outdid the one for their betrothal, the kitcheners and cooks having had far more time for preparation. There was venison, salmon, and even a peacock dressed in its own feathers. The entertainment had the added novelty of a dancing bear which entranced the king. That was followed by dancing and as much as he enjoyed twirling through the steps of the dance, advance and retreat, with his bride, the day could not end soon enough.

The king had nodded off and been removed along with the princesses, when finally the Black Knight leapt to his feet. "To bed with them!" He waved broadly to the musicians. "Pipers, you must lead the way."

Annabella gave a good-natured shrug.

Patrick whispered in her ear, "I shall chase them away as soon as I can." He squeezed her hand, but she was unfazed by the raucous cheers and jokes around them as the queen and the Black Knight followed two pipers up the stairs. In their bed chamber, they were given no time to enjoy the warm glow of the fireplace and candles or the velvet bed hangings. The women, laughing as much as the men, pulled Annabella on the far side of the bed, hidden by bed hangings, but Patrick had his hands full when Alex Boyd, Sir William and the Black Knight joined by even his father and Lord Forbes were unbuttoning his doublet and untying the points that held his chauses. He grabbed onto his braes with both hands. "No!" He laughed. "Leave me a little dignity!"

"Ashamed for us to see what you have?" crowed the Alex Boyd.

"I dinnae think it would interest you, you—" But he got no further in his protestations as they grabbed him by his legs and arms and threw him into the bed. He landed on the bed with a bounce, his legs across Annabella. He quickly rolled off. "Did I hurt you?"

"Nae. Not at all, my husband." The phrase caused her to beam at him, and then she turned to the cheering onlookers and made a shooing motion to them with both arms. "Out!" she shouted and laughed. "Out! We dinnae need you any more."

"Aye, that is truth." Patrick made a ferocious face at the

onlookers as they backed out of the room, several still hooting and laughing. When the door closed behind them, he fell back, took her hand in his, and gave a sigh of profound relief.

“You're sure I didnae hurt you?”

He rolled over on his side and pulled her to him. "At last! Mine, my wife. And I am yours, all I have."

"I liked you from the first moment I saw you all that time ago at the parliament." She cuddled against him. "In my heart, I wanted this for..." She chuckled. "I ken I am nae supposed to tell you that. How long I thought about you."

"That is no bad thing. I am glad of it." He ran urgent hands over her. "You are beautiful. So brave and daring. So tempting. I wanted you so much." He stroked one of her breasts. "Can you blame me?"

"How can I?" She took his hand and in the candle light he could see her blush at her boldness as he slipped it between her thighs, so he could feel she was wet with wanting him. He roller her onto her back so he could bury his face between her breasts, then kissing over her belly and the tawny triangle at her groin, over the velvety skin of her thighs.

He spread her thighs and groaning at the need to keep control. He halted when she gave a brief gasp of pain. He held very still for a moment. "All right?" he whispered.

She nodded her head, eyes wide, arms wound around his waist. She felt so good. He stilled, letting her relax into his intrusion, become accustomed to having him inside her. He eased back oh so slowly. "How is that?” he whispered against her hair.

"Oh." She tightened her arms around him. "Yes."

He closed his eyes and thrust slowly into her again. She moaned softly.

“Good?” he asked, his voice choked with the effort of being soft with her, gentle.

“My love,” she murmured. "My own."

He did it again and felt her body accepting him. *Dear Jesu, he wanted this*.

“Yes," she called out. "Dinnae stop."

And he moved, and he did not stop. Slowly at first, feeling her hips move tentatively to meet him, crying out once again. No longer able to contain his eagerness, he met the thrust with his own, surer now, her body responding so sweetly. He lowered his mouth to hers, explored it for the first time with his tongue and shifted his weight to thrust harder. He could feel the explosion building deep inside him. Beneath him, her body quivered, her back arched. Sweat dripped from his body. Both of them were slick with it.

There was only the passion... only her... only him... She cried out and her body convulsed. His thoughts shattered like crystal...

When he rolled himself off her a bit limply, he called up enough energy to pull her close and kiss the top of her head. "My own..." he murmured. "My sweet lady wife."

Her curling her body against him was all the answer he needed. He sleepily caressed her breasts and the soft curve of her hip, but sleep soon won its way after the long day.

13

Patrick paced back and forth across the bed chamber, shaking his head in frustration. "How can I do this?" he asked his lady wife.

"What choice do we have? Whether you think it wise or nae, the queen has every right to remarry, and she desires that we accompany her to the abbey. She has been all that is kind. We cannae say nae."

"Since she is doing it in secret, that must mean she realizes that Lord Callendar will object. How can we lend our aid to her downfall?"

Annabella rubbed her forehead as though it were aching. "She believes that he will accept a *fait accompli*."

Patrick grabbed up his sword belt and buckled it around his waist. "I pray to all the saints that she is right." He was already clad for riding in heavy wool doublet and boots. He put Annabella's cloak around her shoulders and fasted it with a silver brooch. "I wish you'd stay out of the affair. I dinnae want Lord Callendar blaming you. Let his ire fall on me and the Black Knight."

She laughed, going on her tiptoes to kiss his cheek. "You are a bonnie man, but foolish to even think it."

"Aye. I kent you would say that." He put his arm around her shoulder and they hurried out of their chamber, down the stairs, through the great hall and into the bailey where horses were saddled and waiting. Lady Barbara and Annabella saw the princesses mounted. Patrick raised an eyebrow at the absence of Lady Janet, Callendar's wife and still one of the queen's ladies-in-waiting.

The queen had delayed their departure until Lord Callendar had left the castle for a morning's hunt. Callendar had ordered that the king was to leave the castle only with at least a score of men-at-arms, so the queen had ordered the guards to accompany them. So it was a party of nearly thirty that rode out east toward Cambuskenneth Abbey only a two hour ride to the east on the other side of the River Forth.

The men-at-arms were in a jovial mood, thinking the ride nothing more than an outing. They laughed and jostled, pointing to geese flying overhead in early autumn formations and wondering when they'd see the first snows. They skirted the outer edge of the great Torwood Forest on the higher ground above the Forth. The Cambuskenneth Abbey, set in one of the twists of the River Forth just before it spilled into the salt estuary of the firth, rose in the distance, its spire thrusting high into the sky.

David White, the Abbot of Cambuskenneth Abbey, met them at the doors of the splendid abbey, its huge windows glistening red, green and purple in the midday August sunlight. He was dressed in a resplendent chasuble and heavily jeweled pectoral cross on a heavy gold chain. They heard the singing of a choir from within the abbey.

The abbot led them into the abbey, escorted the queen, the king, and the Black Knight to before the chancel where they knelt as he began the wedding ceremony and wedding mass. Patrick could barely contained his nervous fidgeting and cast sidelong looks at Annabella who was making a strong attempt to look happy for the couple. But her fear was barely below the surface, having absorbed his consternation at this marriage.

He grasped her hand and gave it a squeeze. Whatever happened they would see it through together.

This wedding was long as there were intervals of singing and additional prayers. The king gave his mother's hand to the Black Knight with a giggle that she repressed with a stern look. Sir William produced a ring for the bride and slid it onto her finger as the abbot blessed it and the woman who received it.

There followed more joyous singing and then the blessedly brief nuptial mass. Afterwards there were nervous congratulations, before the abbot led them into a guest house for a hurried feast, for it was essential the king be returned to Stirling Castle before nightfall. The results otherwise did not bare consideration.

When they left although it was well into the afternoon, several hours remained before nightfall. There was a pleasant breeze and light scudding clouds but a nervous disquiet had gone through the company. They all knew that Callendar would be angry at this secret wedding. Even the king and princesses sensed the unease and were silent.

At last the long, weary day was ending as they clattered up the steep incline that led to the castle barbican. They passed through the portcullis and pale gray walls surrounded them where Lord Callendar paced back and forth in the center of the bailey.

Patrick dismounted wearily and lifted Annabella from the saddle, keeping a wary eye on the scowling Callendar.

When they were all dismounted the nobleman marched to face the queen. "*You married!* Did you imagine that I would nae learn of this perfidy! After the protection I've given you!" He turned to glare at the Black Knight who still had a hand on the queen's back after helping her to dismount. "You! You have always been mine enemy. And you think you can gain control of the king through his mother. You are wrong. I shall see to that!" Spittle few from his mouth in his rage.

Patrick heard a footfall behind him and looked over his shoulder. To his horror, a half-circle of pikemen had them trapped, their ten-foot poleaxes lowered for use.

The queen stepped in front of her husband, who took her arm and pulled her back in protest. She held her hands out in appeal. "Lord Callendar, I would not have brought my son to you for safekeeping if I meant to steal him away. I only..." She looked at her new husband, face pallid with fear. "I am so alone since the king died. Surely, you can understand that a woman needs a husband to lend her his strength."

Annabella was squeezing Patrick's arm, mouth open, her face blank with distress. The king had come to stand beside Patrick, looking from his mother to Callendar in bafflement. "I dinnae understand." The princesses were huddled together, wide-eyed.

"Wheesht," he told the lad. "I'll explain later." For once the young king did as he was told.

Callendar raised a clench fist to wave at the queen. "Who can ken what a woman might think, but the Stewarts and their Douglas allies I can never trust. And you've allied yourself with this *man*, so that he can claim to protect his stepson. Are you so stupid, you dinnae ken that is his plan?"

A dozen more men-at-arms, these with swords in hand, had approached from the guardhouse at the gate.

Callendar turned to the pikemen. "You. Escort the Black Knight and his brother to the dungeon. They shall see what comes of betraying my trust."

"No," Queen Joan gasped. She grabbed her husband's arm, but he pried it loose and shook his head.

"Give him time to think, My Lady. I am sure he will come to see we mean him no harm."

Sir William shot his brother a skeptical look but the two men allowed themselves to be herded into the castle. The keep dungeon of the castle had a fearsome reputation, but the men could survive it if... Patrick shook his head. It all depended on Callendar being convinced that his power was not threatened by the queen.

The look Callendar turned on the queen was glacial. "I shall escort you to your new quarters."

That was apparently the last straw for King James who scowled fiercely and ran to block the man's way. "Stop yelling at my mother."

Callendar tilted his head thoughtfully in James's direction. "Aye. If you like, I shall not shout at her." He offered his arm and with a wary, baffled look, Queen Joan took it. "I shall show the lady to her new chamber."

In a low voice, Patrick said to Annabella, "You had best take the king and the princesses to their chambers." He cast an unhappy look at Callendar as he escorted the queen to the King's Building. "I dinnae like this at all."

She nodded. "Your grace, would you help me calm your sisters and take them to their chambers. I fear they are frightened." The king looked unconvinced but went to take Joan's hand. Without someone to sign for her, she had obviously not followed what was happening and had begun silently weeping.

As soon as Annabella had shepherded them out of the bailey yard, Patrick hurried after Callendar and the queen. He found Callendar standing before a strong barred door turning the key in the lock. Two of his men-at-arms, pikes planted at their sides, stood beside the doorway. "Where is the queen?" Patrick demanded, finally losing his temper.

"Where she is safe and where she will stay." Callendar dropped the key into the scrip at his waist. "I'll keep her locked away."

The blood rushed to Patrick's head, the rushing in his head as loud as a high tide. He dropped his hand to his sword. "You'd hold the queen a prisoner?" he shouted.

When one of the men-at-arms dropped the point of a pike before him, Patrick stepped back, startled to his sense. But he could not stand aside while Callendar did this. "You cannae hold the queen prisoner. It is lèse-majesté."

Callendar snorted. "She is no monarch, merely his mother. And she shall come to nae harm. The chamber is comfortable enough. She'll be fed and warm. But there she shall stay as long as need be."

The two men-at-arms both had their pikes lowered, ready to use. Callendar stared at him, eyes narrowed. At the moment, there was nothing he could do. Obviously there was no arguing with Callendar in his present mood. Patrick shook his head. "My lord, this... this is not wise."

"Their marriage was what was not wise. They left me no choice."

Shaking his head again, Patrick trudged back down the stairs. Somehow this must be dealt with but he had no idea how.

14

The next day having given Callendar the night to rethink his actions, Annabella took the princesses to their mother's door. They were turned away. Patrick and Annabella sought out Lady Janet who shook her head dourly when they begged her to intercede with her husband. "I warned the queen against this marriage. Now I fear she must pay the price." When Patrick took the king who made preemptory demand for entry as monarch, they also were firmly told no. The guards stated they took their orders from Lord Callendar and no one else. No entry was allowed. The queen was a prisoner.

Patrick and Annabella wracked their brains what to do. An appeal to Crichton was useless. Even had there been a chance he would intervene, they had no hope that Callendar would listen to him. But they had to try something. Patrick knew that Bishop Cameron had some influence over Callendar, that they were allies to an extent. In the end, they decided that Patrick should go to Glasgow and appeal to the Bishop for aid.

How was this to be done? Callendar was not likely to agree for Patrick to leave his duties with the king, and Patrick was reluctant to leave the young monarch without his protection, but there seemed to be no choice. He would slip away on foot to Stirling Town, there procure a horse and make for Glasgow with all speed. They agreed that this would be done the next day. Boyd declared that he would carry down their weapons in a bundle before first light as he was under less close watch. Patrick could join him, being unarmed and unmounted. If questioned, he would claim an errand in the town, but as it happened no one questioned him as he walked down the cobblestone road.

As promised, Boyd had the horses ready, and it was just the two men riding for Glasgow. In the early autumn, the road to Glasgow was well travelled, but the sight of two well-armed men riding fast made most people give way. They cantered through villages, scattering chickens before them, without slowing but had to make their way through small towns such as Kilsyth and Kirkintilloch at a walk. They kicked their horses to a faster speed in the open road where folk harvesting grain onto carts paused in their work to watch them pass.

Patrick clattered more sedately up Glasgow's bustling High Street. The spires of St. Mungo's Cathedral soared high above the middle of the city, the seat of the Bishop of Glasgow. Both horses were too done to shy at the noise of the market or the shouts of vendors. Neither Patrick nor Alex knew anyone in Glasgow excepting the Bishop so they wended their way through the crowded street to the tall stone keep where Bishop Cameron resided.

The Bishop's Castle had been completed by Bishop Cameron during the late king's reign and showed every sign of that he had put his favor with the king to advantage. A servant led them past silver candle stands that glimmered over silk rugs and well-polished oak furniture suitable for a prince of the church.

John Cameron was sitting near an empty hearth at a table covered with parchments. A stand of candles was on the table beside him. The light gleamed on his bald head, the dark brocade of his gown, and the gold and ruby pectoral cross that hung from his neck. When Patrick and Alex entered the chamber he held out his hand.

"I can spare you a short time," he said as Patrick kissed his ring. "I hope your father is well. And yours, Boyd."

Patrick murmured that he was.

The bishop gestured for Patrick to stand. "How fares the king?"

"As well as can be considering the news of the queen."

"What news of the queen? She is still at Stirling, is she not?"

"She is more than just at Stirling."

"What?" Raising his eyebrows, the bishop waited for Patrick to continue.

"The news has nae reached Glasgow then." Patrick went on to relate how the queen and the Black Knight of Lorne had secretly married, and how in response to this the queen had been confined to a single chamber. He told how the Black Knight and his brother had been thrown into the underground dungeon and the queen's children refused entry to see her. Patrick explained that he believed that only the intercession of the bishop might save the situation from becoming even worse.

Frowning, the bishop listened to the account in obvious anger. "I kent naught of this." He shook his head. "He was to keep me apprised of any developments and Crichton as well. I am working to bring the two men into agreement. This bickering over possession of the king's person must stop. In the meantime, you believe that the queen and the Black Knight are merely confined and nae harmed."

"When I left Stirling that was the case." Patrick cut his eyes to Alex, apprehensive at the tone of Cameron's comments. "The king, as you can imagine, is beside himself at the attack on his mother."

"Och, the king is a child. Of course, he takes his mother's part." He stared at one of the parchments in front of him for a moment, picked up a quill, and neatly penned his signature. "I think I must deal with it, however. If the fighting over the king's person continues, eventually we will have open war. This I shall nae allow. It is to no one's benefit." He got heavily to his feet. "I must prepare to return to deal with this matter. You will return there with all speed and tell Callendar to expect me in two weeks' time."

Dismissed, Patrick and Alex were shown out by a servant who gave them directions to a good inn. As they walked there, the sky still golden with the last light of day, Patrick wondered aloud why they had not been offered the hospitality of the Bishop's Castle. While not quite hostile, Cameron had not greeted them or offered them aid with any great warmth.

Seated on a table in the inn where they had also hired a bed for the night, Alex asked, "How do you think Callendar will react to our appealing to Cameron? We could end up sharing a dungeon with the Stewarts."

Patrick paused as a serving girl put a tray of food on the table. "Cameron and Callendar seemed close when they spoke to me at Stirling. Mayhap even allies. I hope that keeps us out of the dungeon. I've heard stories of what it is like, but if it comes to worse, I think Cameron will have us out." He took a slice of barley bread and used his eating knife to smear it with a good amount of potted herring. He topped it with a slice of pickled onion.

Alex followed suit and took a large bite. "This is nae bad," he said around a mouthful of food. Patrick nodded in agreement. Once their bellies were full, they went to the straw pallets in a common room that they had rented for the night. There was no point in talking about what might happen when they returned to Stirling. They would know soon enough.

❧

At Stirling, Patrick and Alex found the Earl of Avondale with the lord. They were greeted coldly, which was actually better than he had feared.

"So here are the gentlemen-of-the-bedchamber who sneaked away from his duties. By foul stealth." He scowled but showed no sign of his previous rage. "I wonder that you dare to return, Gray."

"I return at Bishop Cameron's bidding, My Lord. And I went to the bishop at the behest of the king who is justly concerned about his mother. Neither command was one I might ignore. The bishop wants the wrangling over possession of the king's person to end."

Callendar raised his eyebrows at Avondale who gave a brief laugh that shook his enormous body.

"He is a presumptuous pup doted on by the queen. But if he spoke with the bishop, I'd hear what his account of that meeting," the earl said.

"The bishop will arrive in a week's time. He told me no more except that he means to see an end of this wrangling." Under Calendar's cold stare, Patrick continued. "I told him of the matter of confining the queen and imprisoning the Black Knight and Sir William. He gave me no hint of his thoughts on that matter."

Callendar nodded but said nothing.

"Bishop Cameron is right about one thing," Avondale put

in. "This arguing over the monarch must end. What is to be done with him in his minority must be settled once and for all. Crichton has some power as the chancellor, and he must be appeased."

"I shall think on it."

Patrick took advantage of Callendar being preoccupied by his discussion with Avondale to take his leave. The earl seemed to be giving Callendar something to think about. Perhaps between Avondale and Cameron he would be brought to his sense, but the fact was he didn't trust Avondale. His father didn't and perhaps that was why. He would try to withhold judgement but the man made his skin crawl. Patrick nudged Alex and they made their way into the keep sharing a grin of relief at having escaped being thrown in the castle dungeon.

Annabella greeted him with a tight embrace and confirmed that there had been no change in the conditions of the queen's imprisonment or that of her new husband.

15

SEPTEMBER 5, 1439

Pacing the bailey in the early morning and wondering why on the eighth day there was still on sign of the bishop, Patrick wished he knew what Cameron had in mind. With the greatest house in Scotland in the hands of a youth barely out of childhood and many such as the earldom of Mar still vacant, only the church could lead them out of this quagmire.

Yes, Cameron said he wanted an end to the disputes but what did that mean for the queen and her freedom? And closely allied as he was with Callendar could the bishop possibly negotiate some peace between that lord and Crichton? If only Pope Nicholas had not called Kennedy to Bologna. He snorted softly. *If wishes were horses then beggars would ride* as he mother ofttimes said.

But the current Black Douglas would not always be an untried youth. Once the king reached a man's estate, they would make the realm once more a place worth living in if they acted together. Both showed every sign of being vigorous leaders. But the realm must be held together until they reached manhood.

He let out a long breath of relief when a short time later a messenger arrived to inform Callendar that a convention was to be held the following day, the tenth day of September, at Cambuskenneth Abbey and urgently requesting his attendance. Patrick could not help but wonder at the calmness with which the man took the bishop's request and the smug smile that briefly broke over his normally grim features.

They rode for the convention in the early afternoon, the cavalcade led by Callendar and Avondale on the huge mount that was required to carry his bulk. The king had been left behind to noisy protests. Patrick rode beside Alex Boyd, William Cranston, and Simon Glendinning, a silent group wondering what they were heading for. Patrick hoped that his father would be at the convention but had had no news of him. And what of the great magnates, the youths Angus and Douglas?

He remembered something he'd heard a priest read from the Bible once: *Woe to thee, O land, when thy king is a child...*

Not only was their king a child, the great magnates were as well.

At the Abbey, Patrick and his friends were relieved to see Lord Gray, whom Patrick only had time to greet briefly. The Earl of Angus accompanied the Earl of Douglas, both grinning and swaggering as they talked to the older men. The grounds of the abbey were a chaos as the retinues of all of the nobles set up encampments. No nobleman travelled without a large retinue of men-at-arms, so although the nobles would be found places in the abbey's guest house, the swarm of their retinues would have to manage for themselves.

Shortly, James of Dalkieth arrived as did the Earl of Huntley, Murray of Tullibardine, Sir Robert Erskine, and Sir Alexander Stewart, generally called 'Bucktooth', adding yet more to the chaos. Alex Boyd growled deep in his throat at the sight of Bucktooth Stewart. The feud between their families had come to blood no more than two months hence, but Patrick squeezed his friend's shoulder. This was no time to look for revenge.

When Crichton rode up with a large retinue, it was a surprise. But, Patrick mused, no long-term peace could be negotiated without his presence.

The abbot, who had performed the marriage of Queen Joan and the Black Knight, was a munificent host to the nobles, so that evening well-fed and comfortable, Patrick and his companions found a quiet corner to speculate whether the convention would somehow find a way to free the queen and the Black Knight as well as his brother and what it might mean for the king.

The next morning, Patrick and his friends were joined by Boyd and some of the supporters of Avondale in the upper part of the large choir area, brightly lit by its long series of stained glass windows. The numerous nobles who had chosen to attend ranged themselves on long pews, many casting suspicious sidelong glances at the others, the glares between Erskine and Alexander Stewart particularly vicious.

Bishop Cameron plodded onto the dais that had been raised in front of the chancel and raised his arms. When he had silence, he intoned a prayer beseeching God's blessings upon their young monarch and all who gave him protection and care. He called down heaven's guidance and benediction on the convention and on their decisions in handling the difficult decisions that faced them. Finally he begged that the Blessed Mother lead them to amity, friendship and cooperation for all here who had the good of the realm in their hearts, most especially to his successor as chancellor of the realm, Lord Crichton.

There were some surprised looks at the Bishop's particular prayers for the man who had succeeded him to power. Patrick raised an eyebrow. Crichton strode to take Cameron's place and hammered once with a mallet on the table. He declared that disorder in the realm was rife, as was to be expected with a child king who was given into the care of his mother. The disunity between himself and Lord Callendar, he declared, was brought about by her scheming and the king's person must be removed from her care. There was a low murmur through the room but Crichton ended that with another bang of his mallet.

Callendar rose and bowed to Crichton. "I desire only amity between the two of us. Together we may work together, with the king safe in my custody while you, as chancellor, ensure the safety of the realm."

Patrick scratched the side of his nose. All this was working out very neatly for someone. How many messengers had made desperate rides between Cameron and the others?

Bishop Cameron rose and added that he was sure that the queen only had the best intentions in regard to her beloved son and monarch, but women had ever been the dupes of Satan. She had sown hatred and dissension between men who had only the good of the realm at heart. They should not blame her for the weakness that was natural to a woman, but must take power from her hands.

Patrick breathed a noiseless snort. So now all the problems since the king's murder were to be laid at Queen Joan's door, Callendar would be substantially enriched, and conveniently the king would out of her hands. Alex cast him a sidelong glance and grimaced.

When Cameron resumed his seat, Crichton said, "The situation must be resolved forthwith. Joan de Beaufort must renounce her right to custody of the king, giving the king into the custody of the Lord Callendar; she must give up her dowry for his maintenance, and confess that all Callendar has done was through zeal for the king's safety. To that end, a representative will be sent to the queen now held in Stirling

Castle to achieve her agreement. Is this proposal to the will of the lords of parliament now present?"

Avondale heaved himself to his feet to so propose. The Earl of Huntley seconded.

"Is there any opposed?" Crichton asked. His eyes widened in surprise when Sir Robert Erskine jumped to his feet.

"The earldom of Mar is rightfully mine!" he shouted. "It was wrongfully seized by the late king and I demand that it be returned as part of any agreement."

Cameron lumbered to his feet. That seizure had been part of his doing and his face was red at the attack. He shook a finger at Erskine. "Alexander Stewart, the late earl, signed patents resigning the earldom to the crown upon his death. That ended your claim to the title."

Erskine shook his fist at the cleric. "I have never seen any such patent. It's a lie from a scheming cleric."

"Enough!" Crichton hammered the mace on the table. "This is nae a matter for this convention to decide." He turned a threatening glare upon Erskine. "Nor is yours the only claim that must be considered, but this is nae the day for it. We must act on the motion already before us."

The church was filled with shouts of agreement.

"Is anyone in opposition?"

When no one spoke up, Lord Gray rose. "My son, Sir Patrick, is on good terms with her grace." Crichton barked out an unpleasant laugh, which Patrick's father ignored as he went on. "Some of you are aware that he is married to her lady-in-waiting, Annabella Forbes, and has spent much time with the royal family. I suggest that we have these proposals drawn up, and he may convey them to her with a full explanation of why signing is strongly to her benefit."

"Do you expect me to believe you are no longer in the queen's pocket, Gray?" Callendar demanded. "Why should I trust you or your son with this? I should throw it in her face myself."

Gray shook his head. "All you would do is make her determined to defy you, no matter the cost. Have you nae already realized that she is a proud woman. She is in the line of kings, the wife of a king and the mother of a king. Yours is nae way to approach her." He pondered Callendar for a moment. "Aye, I desire the best for our queen. I advised her against this marriage, but it is done. Now all she can do is to agree to what Crichton has proposed. I believe Patrick can persuade her to do that. She trusts him. As do I."

Erskine, still on his feet, glowering at the others, said, "Now that is resolved, I demand that we consider my right to the earldom of Mar."

Crichton shook his head. "There is no way that can be resolved today as well as other disputes over claims. We need to consider setting up a council of state to handle various claims and disputes such as yours."

That led to a lengthy dispute involving several hours of shouting as they decided who would be on such a council and what matters they would be authorized to consider and settle. Patrick had doubts whether such a council would be work, but if it reduced some of the recent bloodshed, he could not disagree with appointing one. Not that he was asked.

At last, the convention broke up for the day to convene again the next when they hopefully would have some response from the queen. All reluctance, Patrick took the stairs down to the main level of the church to talk to his father, Crichton, Callendar and Bishop Cameron.

He looked from one to the other in exasperation. "What makes you think she will listen to me? I advised against marrying the Black Knight and she took no heed of it."

"A time locked up can make even the most stubborn

reconsider," Callendar said. "I've seen that she has had a good taste of what could be in store."

Appalled, Patrick demanded, "You haven't harmed her?"

Callendar gave him a look as though he were an idiot. "Of course not. But she has had short rations and no companion to pass the hours she has been locked away. Time to think what might be happening to that new husband of hers as well."

"Aye, I believe she has a true fondness for Stewart." Cameron stroked his chin. "Speak to him first, so you can tell her how he fares. His time in the dungeon, one of the deepest of Stirling Castle I am told, should have made him see reason. And if it has nae, explaining to her that he will never emerge should still give her reason to agree."

Callendar added, "Nor shall she. Either she gives up all claim to the king's person and to her dowry or the two of them stay where they are, locked up. And I have no reason to make their stay comfortable."

"I'll need something in writing to take to her," Patrick said. When Cameron held out a parchment already prepared, Patrick took it with a raised eyebrow. As he had thought, this was planned well in advance, between all of them. He didn't think he father was part of the scheme, but he could not be certain of that either. He quickly read the parchment. It said exactly what Crichton had proposed with room for signatures and seals below. He sighed. "Very well, sirs. I'll leave forthwith."

"One of my men-at-arms will accompany you to convey permission to speak to her husband as well if need be."

So Patrick set out followed by a man-at-arms, riding hard for Stirling Castle. The task he had to do was not at all to his taste, but it must be done.

Annabella greeted him in the bailey yard before even as he dismounted to tell him that there had been no change in the queen's imprisonment. She gasped her dismay when he showed her the agreement from the convention. "She cannae possibly agree to this."

"I fear that she must. No one is going to fight for her to force her release." He gave a grim shake of his head. "Even if some there are some sympathize, now it appears that Crichton and Callendar both are backed by Bishop Cameron. Between the church, the chancellor and the judicial, they hold all the power."

She pursed her lips and rubbed her forehead. "What if she will nae sign it?"

"She must. Somehow I must convince her, or her imprisonment will be even harsher. Callendar made that very clear. I hope if I bring her word of the condition of her husband's imprisonment..." He shrugged.

Down the narrow stairs lit only by a torch the man-at-arms carried and through a heavy door studded with iron, Patrick entered the dungeon deep beneath Stirling Castle. His guide pointed to tiny room open except for thick bars at the front. "Sir James? Sir William?" Patrick called.

"Aye," the Black Knight answered his voice gravelly.

"How do you fare?"

"Our host has nae been generous with his food or his water, but we yet live. We protested being thrown in here, mayhap too vigorously." The Black Knight rose out of a dark corner, limped to the bars, and grasped them with both hands. "More importantly, how fares the queen?"

"She is confined to a chamber and no one allowed to see or to speak to her. But I am to propose a... compromise devised by both Callendar and Crichton."

"Wait." Stewart licked his cracked, dry lips. "Together? They are in agreement?"

Patrick gave a grim nod. "Along with Bishop Cameron." He succinctly described the agreement to the knight's blank amazement. "And if she does nae agree..." Patrick motioned around the dungeon. "If she does nae, then this is your fate."

"The Douglas? What of him? And Angus?"

"They were there. If either of their fathers were still alive —" He made a groan of frustration. "But they are nae and the lads are nae going to attack the Bishop or besiege Stirling for a woman they barely know."

"So she would continue in captivity. They would never put her in here though. I cannae believe that."

"They would also nae release her and her captivity could be more severe. She is denied even her daughters and ladies-in-waiting. What else might they deny her?"

Stewart leaned his head against a bar and cursed softly. After a moment, he said, "Tell her nae to worry about me, but she must protect herself." He raised his head and met Patrick's gaze. "She must accede to their demands."

This was exactly what Patrick had hoped he would hear. Whether it was truly motivated by concern for the queen, he did not care. It might be. But the Black Knight had to have thought in the darkness of the fate of the late king's own brother in exactly such a dungeon, dying of hunger and thirst. Only the queen agreeing to give up her son and with him her power would save the two brothers.

Blowing out a long breath, Patrick clumped up the stairs. Now to persuade the queen. The chamber where she was locked was a small bedchamber in the building of the great hall up a little used staircase. She stood, gaping in surprise when he entered. Her face was drawn and her silk dress wrinkled. When the door closed behind him, she frantically bade him tell her of her husband's fate. When Patrick assured her that he had suffered little harm, she sank onto a chair and buried her face in her hands.

"I should have learned that there is no one who will not betray you. It is a hard lesson, Sir Patrick. Very hard. It cost me..." Her eyes when she looked put were gleaming with tears, but she looked away, too proud to let them fall. "My lord king and now my dear love, all of us betrayed by those we trusted."

"Stewart and his brother are not dead yet, Your Grace, and you can save them." He took the folded parchment out of his scrip and offered it. "But please I beg that you believe none of this was my doing."

After she read the document, she leaned back, eyes closed and her face even paler than before. "They would take everything from me."

He knelt and looked up into her eyes. "Not everything, Your Grace. Your husband will live and be free as will you. You can regroup and gather allies. And your son will be safe. There will never be a day when I will not guard him with my very life."

She slowly nodded and then re-read the parchment in her hands. "I suppose there are threats they did not put in this document."

"That you and your husband will never be free if you do nae sign." Patrick shook his head. "I dinnae think they would dare harm you, Your Grace. Your connections in England guarantee that, but your confinement could be harsher. But how long will the Black Knight and his brother live? Lack of food and water would soon dispose of them, without Callendar lifting a finger."

When Queen Joan nodded, her mouth was nothing more than a thin white line. "Can you witness this, Sir Patrick? Take it with all speed to my captors, but pray speak to Bishop Cameron. He has betrayed me as well, but I do not think he would sign this and not keep his word. So tell him I still trust him that much. He must swear that husband will be released."

Two days later, the agreement signed by all parties, the

queen, her husband, his brother, her ladies-in-waiting, and her daughters prepared to depart Stirling, escorted by the Earl of Angus and his men-at-arms. He had once again put the impregnable Dunbar Castle at her disposal.

Patrick and Annabella had spent one last night together with no way of knowing when they would be rejoined. In the courtyard, she unabashedly hugged him and gave him a passionate goodbye kiss. She had no choice but to go with the queen as was her duty. Patrick's duty lay with the king at Stirling Castle. At least for a while, there might be something like peace in the kingdom.

Dry-eyed, the king bade his mother goodbye, kissed his sisters as she instructed, and watched them ride out the gate. Then, back straight as a blade, turned his gaze toward Callendar. He rubbed the side of his nose, eyes narrowed. But when Callendar looked down at him, a small, possessive smile on his lips, the king turned his back. "I smelled the cooks baking sweets, and they always spare me some." He smiled sweetly at Patrick. "They like me quite well."

16

APRIL 1440

The king's marked distaste for his guardian was little problem. The man seemed willing enough to leave the lad to his gentlemen-of-the-bedchamber and tutors. The tutors had more than a few complaints about the king's tendency to skip his lessons at every chance, but keeping up with the fast growing nine-year-old kept his gentlemen busy.

Most of the time spent at archery, quarterstaff and sword lessons was with Patrick. But Alex Boyd, William Cranston, and Simon Glendenning took turns keeping up with the active monarch when he was sledging at hurlyhackit or further abroad for hawking, hunting, or just taking his horse for a gallop. Callendar's son, only a year older than James, often joined them and to Patrick's surprise the two boys got on well, even became friends. Any venture outside the castle walls required a full score of men-at-arms, as Callendar had no intention of risking someone stealing the king from his keeping. The men-at-arms had strict orders not to let the monarch out of their sight or let anyone not of the castle near him, but racing after the king kept them all on their toes.

Most of Scotland was at an uneasy peace. No more of Avondale or Crichton were seen at Stirling though messengers from both arrived several times. Try as he might, Patrick could learn nothing of what the three men were planning. Word came from Loch Lomond that Sir John Colquhoun, governor of Dumbarton Castle, had accepted a treacherous invitation from Lachlan Maclean and Murdoch Gibson to meet with them to settle a dispute at Inchmarten. There, to settle a longstanding feud, they attacked him and his men and murdered him, but the Chancellor sent no word of taking action, so a sort of peace continued.

When news came from Dunbar Castle in the spring, it was in Annabella's hand with word that made Patrick's heart race. The queen invited him to come to Dunbar for the celebration of Princess Joan to the Earl of Angus. She eagerly wanted a personal accounting of how her son fared and would welcome his company. Patrick paced the ramparts that night, half sick with apprehension that Callendar would prevent his going.

He was eager to make the trip to Dunbar Castle to see Annabella. Alex complained that he was as grumpy as a bear with a sore paw, but he missed his wife. Somehow they must devise a way to be together, but for now he would settle for sending a few hours in her arms. It took an hour of convincing after he received the invitation, but Callendar finally agreed that a personal visit from Patrick to assure the queen that the king was doing well might prevent some future rebellion from the her or her supporters. In truth, Patrick did believe that the young king and his realm had enough problems without the queen warring with Callendar, however much he disliked the man.

Patrick had never before had any reason to go to the great fortress of Dunbar Castle, one of the strongest in all of Scotland. Dunbar, on the east coast of Lothian, was a substantial ride across the Firth of Forth and past the Lammermuir Hills down to the sea and past the mouth of the Tyne. On huge stone outcroppings, the most amazing fortress Patrick had ever laid eyes upon stood before him. Built on perpendicular rocks that jutted out from the sea, each portion was reached only by narrow covered bridges. The castle was impregnable. It would make capturing Stirling look like child's play, not that it had done the Earl of Dunbar any good. The earl had been stripped of his title and was in exile, while the Earl of Angus or rather his guardian controlled this fortress and for the moment used it for the safekeeping of the queen and her daughters.

Only the gatehouse tower was on land where he was forced to tarry for a while. Because no message had come ahead of him, he waited until his entry was approved by the queen. But once his entry was approved, he went through the long bridge and might almost have been at sea, so cut off was the castle from the mainland.

Annabella rushed to greet him, and he held her tight, kissed her soundly and then pushed her back so he could look her up and down.

"You look bonnie, my love." He pulled her into his arms for another kiss. "When can we steal a moment alone?"

She laughed and pulled him into the chamber to greet the queen and the princesses. "Soon, My Lord Husband. Now behave."

He had to admit that she looked like a rose in full bloom, her cheeks rosy with color and she still had the sprinkling of freckles across her nose that he had always found charming.

The queen welcomed him warmly, immediately asking after her son who had sent her his greetings. She explained that the earl and his guardian and uncle, Sir William Hay of Yester, would join them on the morrow for the betrothal for Angus's Tantallon Castle was only a short ride away.

Patrick was able to tell the queen all that the king was doing, how fast he was growing, and his continued boredom with his lessons, which made the queen shake her head with a fond smile. She had to hear how he did with the bow, the quarterstaff and the sword and how he did with his hawking. All of those, Patrick agreed, were much more to James's taste. When the queen had heard every last detail he could think of to tell her, Mary played a tune on the harp while little seven-year-old Eleanor sang a song in French for them. He noticed that Joan seemed to be keeping time to the music, surprising since he knew she could not hear.

The queen nodded when she saw him watching the girl. "She seems to feel the music somehow, although I know she cannot hear it. Her father hired a tutor from Milan, you see, and he has taught her talk with her hands most amazingly." She shook her head. "I feared she would have a terrible life when we discovered she could not hear, but not at all. We've brought up a lady's maid as her companion who signs so when she marries the earl or where ever she goes, she will always have someone who understands the words she makes with her fingers."

Joan seemed to sense they were talking about her and glanced their way, but then she turned back to her sister who motioned for her to put her hand on the harp.

At last it was bedtime, he discovered that all the princesses and Annabella had their bedchambers in the most seaward tower across a bridge that was nearly seventy feet in length. The queen assured him with a knowledgeable smile that Annabella's chamber was separate from the children's.

He escorted the princesses most formally, offering his arms to the younger ones and giving them fits of giggles. He waited less than patiently in the hall while Annabella saw that the girls were settled in their chambers. When he escorted her up the next story to hers, she pulled him inside and closed the door behind them.

Before she could look around to be sure all was prepared for their comfort, he had her in his arms. "Oh, hen. At last." He kissed her and kissed her again. "It has been so long." Then words were superfluous.

If neither slept that night, they had no complaint. The next day was a frenzy of activity. Young red-haired Angus arrived with his very dignified uncle and fifty men-at-arms at midmorning. In the afternoon, after the guests were refreshed, the betrothal was signed with all appropriate ceremony. Then the queen outdid herself with the banquet, with every sort of food and acrobats, a jester and a dancing bear for entertainment between the fifteen courses.

Patrick had no interest in the food except to see that his wife had the choicest morsels from his knife. As for entertainment, the evening dragged on until he was convinced they would never have the chance to escape to her bedchamber and share the delights of her bed. But at last they were alone.

Coming together, their clothes were shed with no care for damage. Sprawled together, her hands and mouth were as busy as his own. The delight of her warm body in his embrace, the urgency of her kisses, the press of her body against his, he panted and caressed, ecstatic that her need matched his.

Afterwards, they lay holding each other in languid bliss, not speaking. It had been worth the wait, would be worth yet more. But how long? He pulled her head onto his shoulder, and lazily twined his fingers in her long hair, plotting how he could free them from duties except this to each other.

The parting the next morning was direly inescapable, matched in its gloom by the drizzle that fell, wetting him through as he began the sixty-mile ride back to Stirling and to his obligation to the king.

James was delighted to see him and if he was less delighted with the clothes his mother had sent as a gift, he was too courteous a boy to say so. He grew so fast, keeping him suitably clothed made Callendar groan and complain, but he'd not chance being accused of ill-treating his sovereign lord.

In the meantime, Patrick wracked his head with schemes and ideas of how to arrange to have his wife nearer to him. Two weeks after his return, he approached his young liege lord for permission to visit his own lands in Aberdeen, a short ride north of Inverbervie. The king reluctantly consented, though it was only a courteous formality. Real permission came from Lord Callendar who admitted that inspection of his lands might be a necessity. He warned however that he had no intention of relieving Patrick of his duty of service to the king.

So he was off the next morning for Aberdeen, borrowing two of Callendar's men-at-arms, for traveling alone was an invitation to be attacked. It was a good two-day ride through Perth and Dundee. He cut inland, skirting Arbroath where the Scots had for good and all declared they would never be ruled by the English, and then straight north.

The castle had been that of one of his uncles and since it was far from his father's lands was a place he'd visited only twice. It was easy to find just up a steep-sided promontory from a tiny village dominated the spire of a church. He was pleased with the place. The escarpment was steep but topped with a grassy slope beyond the small castle's walls. Within sight was the narrow ribbon of Bervie Water before it reached the North Sea.

At the top of the steep slope in a spot that would be good for defense stood the modest, square, stone keep within a high courtyard wall. A tiny ribbon of smoke twined from the chimney, but there was no sign of occupation otherwise although he'd been told a man-at-arms served as caretaker for the place. At the closed gate, he cupped his hand to his mouth and bellowed as loudly as he could, "Hoi! The house!" He shouted twice more before there was an answer.

"Who goes? What's the to-do?"

Patrick shouted that it was the master of the house come to inspect his property. After considerable scraping and thumping, the gate was opened by a grizzled, elderly retainer. The man introduced himself as Donald MacCallan. He had indeed been a man-at-arms for Patrick's uncle and now he and his son saw that the place did not fall into wrack and ruin. The small stables looked in good repair, so while the men-at-arms took the horses to stable, he followed MacCallan over a narrow wooden gangplank that bridged a defensive gap. The man explained that the gangplank was run out from within the walls rather than a more complicated drawbridge. It was a simple defense but would be effective in an attack that breached the outer wall.

Pausing, he examining the tower. It had narrow arrow slits for windows on the ground floor, also a good defense. The next three levels had arched windows wide enough to use either for archery or for heaving stones down on attackers. For a small keep, the defenses were adequate.

The gangplank creaking loudly beneath their weight as they crossed made him think he might make a few repairs. A quick glance down the six foot drop where sharp rocks lined the bottom of the gap assured him that a fall would be highly unpleasant. MacCallan shoved open the oak plank door both studded and banded with iron. He motioned Patrick to enter ahead of him with a courteous bob, so Patrick passed through the entry passage in the eight-foot-thick walls.

Patrick stepped into the main hall of his home-to-be. It

would be a comfortable hall with ample room for bedding for retainers although at the moment the stone-slab floor was nude of rushes. Trestles were stacked against one wall next to long boards that would form tables. A rough stone fireplace a full ten-feet wide at the far end would make the large room welcoming on winter nights. Near the fireplace was a bundle of furs that Patrick thought must serve MacCallan as a bed. A circular stair in one corner went both up and down.

"Will you be biding, Sir Patrick?" MacCallan asked. "It has been a long time since there was a proper laird in the keep. It would comfort villagers to have a place to retire to if we were attacked."

Patrick went down the steps as he said, "Not for a time. My duties keep me with the king. But one day I hope to bring my lady wife to bide here, and we have a chance to make a home here." He grinned "I would nae even mind if we filled the place with bairns. It seems a pleasant and secure place for a family."

The vaulted lower level could be used as a dungeon if it were needed but instead was full of dusty stacks of trestles and kists that might well hold old clothes. In the middle was the cover of a well. "Good." Water if they should ever be attacked would not be a problem though it would not be a convenient location for carrying water to fight a fire.

He followed MacCallan up to the second floor where there was a small room that could serve as a lady's solar and a bedroom with a massive box bed taking up much of the space. A door led to a garderoom cut into the thick wall for necessary sanitation. The floors above served as storage space and armory with space that might serve for bed chambers for children when he had them. For if they had a child, the queen would be hard pressed to deny Annabella's right to her own home.

MacCallan had several rabbits hung that he roasted over a

fire. They all managed well enough for the night. Patrick decided that there was nothing more he could do for the nonce, but Kinnett Castle would do well once it had more furnishings and a woman's touch to warm it. He gave MacCallan a merk as a reward for his good service and promised to take up residence as soon as his duties allowed.

17

OCTOBER 1440

It was the king's tenth birthday. After giving several days' thought to what would be a gift that the monarch would enjoy, he decided it was time for the lad to have more than a blunted blade. James was entranced with it, sitting cross legged on in a window nook, running a cloth over hilt while Patrick sat at a table nearby writing a letter to Annabella. "One day I shall use it against my enemies," the king said softly. "It is wonderful."

"Hopefully you will have few enemies who need killing, Your Grace."

James looked at him for a long moment as though he were dense and then went back to polishing his new sword. "All kings have enemies."

Patrick shook his head. It was better not to ask—

The thought was broken off when Callendar threw open the door and entered. He smiled at James and nodded to Patrick. "Your Grace, I have saved a treat to tell you about for your birthday."

Patrick raised his eyebrow. The man rarely made the

trouble of seeking out the king much less planning a treat for him.

Callendar gave a preemptory wave of his hand at Patrick, so Patrick rose, wondering what the man could possibly be up to. The lord placed a finely written parchment on the table. "Look. It is an invitation to William, Earl of Douglas and his brother David to join you for a dinner celebration. We will travel to Edinburgh. Crichton suggested the idea and I thought it seemed a fine one. You and the Earl are nae so far apart in age. It would be wise for the two of you to become friends, the king and the head of the most powerful house in the land."

James put the sword down on the seat and came over, giving Callendar a wary look, but his face brightened when he read the invitation. "Aye, I remember them I think from the day of my coronation. We rode together and he had a braw horse."

"Good. Good." Callendar patted the king's shoulder, something Patrick had never seen him do before. "The invitation should be over your signature. That will make it even more of an honor for them."

Patrick's mind was spinning as the king sat in Patrick's place and carefully penned his signature. "So this celebration will be in Edinburgh?"

"Aye, that is what I said," Callendar said brusquely as he picked up the document with the king's signature now on it. He headed for the door.

"And this was Crichton's idea?" Patrick asked, but Callendar closed the door behind him without bothering to answer. Patrick chewed on his lip, staring at the closed door. The king had not been in Edinburgh since Patrick had helped steal him out from Crichton's grasp.

Could it be some plot of Crichton's to get the king back into his keeping? But he had been well rewarded for giving the king to Callendar with being confirmed as Chancellor and a substantial stipend for his own upkeep. Besides, Callendar would hardly agree unless he had assurances that no such scheme was afoot. So... what could be the reason for this sudden change? The two men did nothing unless it was to their benefit.

He would have the begging friar they used for carrying messages accompany them to Edinburgh in case something came of his suspicions. He could hope that Callendar had realized he should try to make a friend of the king, that it was nothing. He had no confidence of it.

18

NOVEMBER 1440

"Sir Patrick, look. There they are." King James pointed. Sitting on the top edge of the parapet where he'd climbed, he lean out dangerously far to scan the road below.

A fine drizzle had begun to fall and the stone was slick. Patrick bit his tongue on telling the king to be careful or he'd fall and break his royal neck. Such warnings only made him more daring. Instead, he leaned a hand on the merlon and craned to catch sight of the expected party of riders. Down the hill, he could just make out a flutter of banners above a group of horsemen. It was only a dozen for Douglas's tail of at least a hundred men had to be left behind, too many to be accommodated at the castle.

Patrick suspected they could have been, but probably Callendar did not trust so many men-at-arms within his walls.

The king hammered his heels on the outside of the parapet where he was perched. "I wish they might stay for more than a day. Why did Callendar invite them just for a dinner? Since they've come all the way to Edinburgh, they might stay for a few days."

Patrick rubbed his chin. As much as he'd tried, his probing had obtained no explanation of this invitation to the Earl of Douglas and his younger brother to dine with the king. Every question had been met with more generalities that the dinner would settle differences between the crown and the powerful house of Douglas. When Patrick asked what differences those were since he knew of none, Crichton still waved the question away.

"I suppose he had a reason." He turned and looked his young king up and down. "You should brush yourself off. You dinnae want to look like a beggar lad before the Earl of Douglas."

James looked down in surprise at his doublet smeared with dust from his clambering onto every high point he could find. "Och, aye. I suppose that I do." He swung his feet around to jump down. "Do they dress very bonnie, do you ken? They were there when I was crowned, but that was a long time ago."

Patrick smiled as he let the king precede him to the narrow stairway to the royal chambers. "The Douglas seemed a bit of a peacock when I saw him, aye. Sixteen years old now, I suppose, so probably thinks himself a man full grown."

"David is younger though. He is only a little older than I. We could ride out to do some hawking if they stayed a few days."

"Your hawks are at Stirling Castle. Forbye, the weather is too cold for it."

James grumbled at being denied a hawking expedition as he preceded Patrick down the four flights of stairs of David's tower and through the upper yard into the lower. By that time James had exhausted the subject of the abuse he had suffered at not being allowed to bring his own falcon and that a deer hunt would be a fine sport for their guests.

When they rounded the corner, the visitors were clattering through the castle gates, a cluster of silk and velvet and plumed, bejeweled bonnets with outriders in polished steel. Over their heads a huge banner whipped back and forth in the damp wind, emblazoned with the crowned heart of the Black Douglas.

"Hurrah!" shouted James, waving furiously. "They're here."

The Earl of Douglas, rangy as ever, thick waves of black hair falling past his high collar, in the lead grinned as he doffed his bonnet and swung from the saddle. Another dark-haired lad of about twelve years followed suit, Douglas's brother David. Patrick would not have recognized him, he'd grown so much taller since the king's coronation.

All of the men-at-arms wore the colors of Crichton. Douglas's men were lodged at Crichton's castle where they'd stopped on the way.

James hurried to the brothers, chattering as he went. "I am so glad you have come. I'm sure we shall be great friends. Next time, I swear you must stay longer. This only staying for a day is a shame."

Douglas laughed as he bowed. "Mayhap you will bring your court to my own Threave Castle when you have come into your power, Your Grace, though it is nothing in size to this Edinburgh."

"How many castles do you have? Many I suppose. Everyone says so." He glanced at Patrick. "Is that not so, Sir Patrick?"

"Aye, that is so."

"My tutor made me read that long, long, long poem by Barbour and it was all about how the Douglas saved my ancestor, King Robert. It was a braw story but too long." He cocked his head and studied the brothers. "You look like mayhap you could fight, too, when you are older."

Patrick couldn't help the laugh that burst out but James gave him a reproachful look, since he never liked being laughed at. Not that Patrick could blame him. “My apologies, Your Grace. I just hope that we have no such war as King Robert the Great had to fight.”

“No, but I do well at the list,” Douglas said, his grin widening. “I plan on a tourney next summer and inviting knights from France and mayhap even England.”

David was twitching with eagerness and put in, “By then I shall be old enough to ride at the tilt as well!”

Callendar had followed them out. He marched stolidly up but put a smile on his face at the last moment. “Your Grace, our guests have had a long ride. Let us show them to their chamber so they can remove the dust of the road before dinner.” He motioned to the way to the upper yard. “Please, My Lords, be welcome.”

The Earl smiled courteously at Crichton as he dismounted and joined them. "Lord Crichton gave us such welcome at his castle, we are hardly wearied at all, but removing the dust of the road would be welcome."

“Aye, let us go in.” James said. He turned and started to bolt toward the tower but checked himself so he could keep pace with the Douglas. “You must tell me all about riding at the list. Do you like it? Have you ever been in a tourney?”

“Only one because we do nae have so many here in Scotland, but I plan to change that. I do like it. It takes much practice with the lance. Have you practiced with that yet?”

The king frowned. "Only a little. Sir Patrick says I need to be larger to handle one, but I'm growing fast."

“Oh, Your Grace, you should see my new courser,” David exclaimed. “I wanted to bring him but the stable master said he was still too young for such a long ride.”

They chatted about tourneys until they reached a chamber that was given over to the Douglases. When James wanted to stay to talk, Crichton who had followed along silently reminded him that he must change his clothes for the banquet, so he reluctantly trudged to his own chamber. Patrick followed to do the same, for it was a state banquet to be held, the first of the young king's reign.

He and Alex had been given their old chamber, high in the tower that was, as usual, cold as a witch's tit, but he stripped, tossed his clothes in a basket and hung his sword on a peg. He washed his face, hands, arms, legs with a soapy rag, rinsed and toweled off. He donned his best doublet, green silk edged with marten, a wedding gift from his father. Then he went to attend the king who had splendid new attire for the occasion, a rarity in itself, blue silk that brought out the startling blue of his eyes.

Patrick entered the great hall through a side door and went to stand at his assigned place at the end of a long linen-draped side table set with pewter trenchers. The head table on the dais was reserved for the king, his guests, and the men of state. The hall was already redolent with the scent of roasted meat, savory herbs, and fresh baked bread and his stomach grumbled. The tables were lit with dozens of silver candle stands and torches high on the columns reflected light so only a few shadows hid in the corners.

The gray walls were hung with banners, the great lion rampant of the King of Scots, the crowned red heart of the Earl of Douglas, the starred banner of one of the other Douglases as well as the banners of Crichton and Callendar. A cheery fire crackled in the wide hearth.

The men-at-arms, a great many of them all with pike in hand, stood guard at the doors. When Boyd strolled in Patrick's direction, a page pointed to a place half-way down from the head of the table. He glanced toward Patrick and shrugged. Scanning the rest of the men taking their places, Patrick realized that not one was of the group that had arrived with the young earl, but it had been a small group indeed. Lord Haliburton and Lord Borthwick, both with lands near Edinburgh and allies of Callendar, were taking their seats.

At the center of the table behind places reserved for the principals stood four trumpeters, resplendent in royal livery. At a wave from the castle steward, they raised their horns and blasted a loud flourish. The doors were thrown open and the Earl of Douglas, all scarlet velvet and white silk, strode behind two heralds. Next to him, the king was waving his hands about as he chattered to the earl's young brother. It was a shame Callendar had chosen not to bring his own son who would have enjoyed the show, Patrick thought.

Then came James Douglas of Avondale, as fat as ever, red-faced, and sweating through his silk doublet, whom Patrick had not even known was in Edinburgh. Why was Avondale there? Invited, Patrick supposed, but an odd choice. Next to Avondale was his oldest son, William Douglas, a man grown at twenty years, lean as his father was fat, dark-haired, a crooked, unpleasant smile, his face marred by pustules. Callendar and Crichton took up the rear of the little procession and with them next to his hatchet-faced father, the Thane of Glamis, Alexander Lyon walked, his gazed fixed on his feet. Patrick wondered what had Lyon looking so dour. Perhaps he'd had a scold from his father for the amount of time and money he spent whoring.

King James took his seat in a throne-liked chair with the Earl of Douglas on one side and young David on the other. He threw back his head to laugh at something David said, and Patrick had to smile. With the king so well entertained, Patrick could relax.

There was a brief blessing from a priest Patrick did not recognize and then Crichton, beside the young David, rose, gave a toast to the earl, bowed, and drank to him. Patrick raised an eyebrow when Alex Lyon starred glumly into his cup and did not join in the toast. But Avondale was smiling amiably, his face dripping with sweat, and his son seemed to be hiding a smirk as they sat on one side of the earl. Callendar sat with a self-satisfied look, like a cat that got into the creamery.

When Avondale's son caught his eye, Patrick found it hard to tear his gaze from him. What gave his lean, dark face such a hungry look? It made the back of Patrick's neck twitch, but he shrugged it off and reached for his cup. A page filled it with malmsey that gave up a rich scent. Tonight, he intended to enjoy himself while the king did the same. To the devil worrying what Avondale and his dark-faced son might be up to.

In the musicians' gallery above, fiddlers and harpers began to play. Beaming, the Earl of Douglas gave his thanks for being invited to dine with the king, and raised his cup high in a toast. The feasting began when pages carried in platters, several whole geese stuffed with chestnuts, a huge salmon served with onions and beans, and apples cooked in wine were the first course.

Patrick speared a slice of goose dripping with gravy and dropped it onto his trencher, his mouth watering. His stomach grumbled as he sliced into it and set to.

The man-at-arms on his left leaned close and said, "Someone told me that when the Earl of Avondale was on his way to Edinburgh, he asked a peasant he met, 'Do you think I shall be able to enter the gate?' Och, he meant to ask whether he would reach the city before the gates closed. But the man told him, 'Certes, you will, My Lord. A cartload of hay can fit through. I'm sure you will fit, too.'"

Patrick sputtered into his cup. It was an old joke, but well done turned on the unpleasant Earl of Avondale. That made it new again. He eyed the earl who had never had a good word for anyone that Patrick ever heard. "He got through, but I suspect barely."

His companion brayed a laugh. When Patrick looked back toward the high table, Callendar was staring at him. There was nothing wrong with laughing and enjoying himself, but he hid his grin behind his cup. Still Callendar stared at him and then caught Crichton's eye, who looked his way as well.

Patrick strained to hear what was being said at the head of the table over the music, roar of the fire, clatter of pewter plates and cups, and the gabble of dozens of men talking. The king's piping voice carried as he chattered about when he would be free to do as he pleased, and that he would ride and tourney with his Douglas cousins. David said that they would have to have feasts like this every day. Perhaps they would, Patrick thought. Perhaps they would.

He turned his attention to his companions talk about Bishop Cameron's new additions to Saint Mungo's Cathedral in Glasgow and plans for defense if the English should invade. More courses were carried in, a whole roast boar, a huge eel pie, and bowls of rose pudding with sweet wafers.

James was grinning and chattering to young David more than he ate, and the earl was amiably nodding as the younger boys rattled on. Crichton gave no more toasts but picked at his food, looking out over the hall with hooded eyes. James of Avondale tore the meat from the leg of a goose with his teeth, but his son was looking about still with that odd sneer, except when he drank from his wine cup. Between the courses acrobats did cartwheels and built a human pyramid. Another course was carried in that Patrick waved away, already having had a surfeit. Even his companions had grown quiet, no more japes as the many cups of wine made them muzzy headed.

Then Callendar motioned to a herald. The music ceased.

The doors of the hall were thrown open with a crash. Two drummers stepped through and took up a slow, pounding beat so heavy the air thrummed with it. Four servitors dressed in black robes bore in on their shoulders a huge silver platter at least six feet across. They marched, grim faced and solemn. The hall fell silent, except for that dreadful drum beat.

Patrick leaned forward, breath caught in his throat. On the platter was the massive head of a black bull with wide pointed horns. In the platter, blood puddled around it, still fresh and crimson. Its eyeballs seemed to glare beneath the shaggy hair, matted with gore. Someone gasped. Patrick went icy cold with horror.

The servitors marched step by slow step to the drum beat towards the high table.

James gaped at them. Between the beats of the drum, his voice piped up, "What is that horrible thing? Take it away!"

David leaned forward, puzzled, mouth agape, but his brother sat unmoving. The earl watched, tight faced but eyes wide, the approach of the men, shuffling under the weight of their burden. Patrick was sure the lad knew what this gory spectacle meant.

Patrick looked around the room for some help, someone to stop whatever was about to happen. Whose death did that thing signify?

Avondale's son knew. A grin had spread across his face. Avondale was nodding, silent and satisfied.

The servants grunted as they hefted the heavy platter high and then slammed it onto the table, right in front of the earl. Blood splashed onto the white table linen.

The drumbeat stopped. The only sound in the room was a long hiss of indrawn breath from Patrick and the thump of the guard's feet as spread out across the room. Metal scraped as they drew their swords. The men-at-arms at the doors dropped their pikes into battle position with a clatter.

James slowly stood, holding onto the earl's arm. He might

not know exactly what it all meant, but it was obviously something awful.

Callendar rose. "Treason," he intoned. "You, My Lord Earl, have proposed treason against your liege lord, and here is the reward you have earned."

"No!" The Earl of Douglas rose to his feet, knocking his chair over with a crash, his eating knife clutched in his hand. "I have not. Never."

David Douglas stared blankly at Callendar. "What is it? What treason?"

"Stop this." James scowled but his voice trembled. "What do you mean? We were... We were just talking. They're my friends, my cousins."

Patrick gripped his hands into fists, desperate to do something. But there was nothing to be done. He didn't even have a sword. No one wore a sword to dine at the king's table, and he couldn't have used it if he'd had one. The men-at-arms were all loyal to Callendar and Crichton. The king was in their charge.

"Guards, seize the two miscreants. Take them out to be held for their trial and sentence."

Chairs scrapped and clattered as everyone got to their feet, moving warily. Patrick was breathing as fast as if he had just run a race. His ears thumped with his rushing pulse, but his feet seemed glued in place.

Men-at-arms were already moving toward the two young Douglases. David, blank-faced with confusion, let them pull him from his chair and shove him towards the door.

The earl jerked away from two men who grabbed at his arms, shouting wordlessly with indignation. He slashed at the first. The man swung. Douglas ducked the blow and sank his eating knife into the guard's hand. The second pulled back his fist and landed a blow square in Douglas's face. The earl fell backward across the table, blood splattering from his nose. His small blade skittered across the floor.

James shouted, "Stop! Stop this now!" He grabbed Douglas's arm, but the two hard-faced men jerked the earl from his grasp.

Douglass struggled in their grasp. One of them wrenched his hand up behind his back. Douglas yelped but still thrashed to get free. They dragged him, blood dripping down his face, resisting every step, out the door.

The entire room was silent. Then James grabbed Callendar's arm. "Stop. You cannot do this." Callendar turned away, no more bothered than if the boy had been an annoying fly.

Patrick shoved his way through the stunned guests, who seemed not to know what to do. They looked this way and that, many open-mouthed. Patrick wove his way past them; he had to reach the king.

Crichton was patting James on the shoulder. "Calm yourself, Your Grace. They were plotting to seize the throne. They would have murdered you. Remember your father's death. That was what they planned for you."

"No, William likes me." James backed away from Crichton, shaking his head. "And David. He's just a lad. Like me. They weren't doing anything wrong."

"We have no time for this nonsense." Callendar pointed one by one as he called out names. "Avondale. Glamis. Haliburton. Borthwick. With us. And Crichton you bring... His Grace." He turned on his heel and marched toward the door where the men-at-arms had exited. The others hurried after them, and a low buzz of dismay and speculation filled the room.

He wasn't invited, but Patrick was not about to let the king out of his sight, so he simply joined them. He walked beside James who was staring hard at Callendar's back.

In a small side chamber, the earl of Douglas was gripped

between two men-at-arms. His nose was bleeding. A split in his lip from a blow dribbled blood down his chin. His face was a mask of rage, but he now longer struggled, whether from the blow that had bloodied him or the arm viciously twisted behind him, Patrick couldn't tell. The younger boy stood still and silent, pale-faced, eyes darting from one man to another for help.

Callendar motioned to the men accompanying them to join him facing the prisoners. "Sirs, as Judiciar of Scotland, I declare that we have here a sufficiency of the council of state to try these traitors, and so we shall do." There was a murmur of agreement.

"As Chancellor, I declare that is true and we can so judge," Crichton put in.

Callendar continued in rote tone that sounded rehearsed, "You, William Douglas and David Douglas, are charged with high treason. William Douglas has claimed that the throne of Scotland is his by rights and that his brother is his heir. They have sought allies in both Scotland and abroad for their treason. This perfidy endangers our sworn liege lord and the kingdom. Do you have any answer to this charge?"

"It's a lie! I never did that." The young earl looked at the men ranged around him. His face was red with outrage. "You ken that I never did. How could I? My father is hardly cold in his grave."

"Has any member of the council aught to add?"

"Stop this!" James threw himself in front of the Callendar. He rubbed away some tears with the heel of his hand. "You won't harm them, I tell you. You cannot. I forbid it."

Avondale shook his huge head. "None who value our liege lord's life could deny the charges."

Callendar nodded to Crichton who pointed a finger at the two brothers. "As Chancellor of the Realm, I declare you William Douglas, Earl of Douglas, and you, David Douglas, are guilty of high treason. You will be taken from here to the place of execution and there each of you will have your head struck from your body. And may God have mercy upon your souls."

David gave a strangled, "No..."

Douglas looked from one to the other, teeth bared in a snarl. The guard jerked his arm even higher and the young earl choked down a yelp of pain. He closed his eyes then and seemed to gather himself. "I am guilty of no wrong and you —" His voice broke. "—you are murderers."

The two men-at-arms wrestled him, no longer resisting, toward the door and out. David whimpered as the men-at-arms dragged him away.

"Stop them!" James grabbed Patrick's arm and shook it. "I told them no. They can't. I am the king, and I said no!"

It was hopeless, but Patrick did his best. Forcing his voice to sound calm, he stepped forward face Callendar. "You heard the king. It is a royal command."

Callendar's voice would have cut glass. "The king is a minor and has no voice in matters of state or of law. Our duty is to execute the traitors. This we shall do."

James leapt in front of Callendar, his hands gripped in fists so tight his knuckles were white.. "You... You murderer. You... You..."

"Someone remove the king." He glanced at Avondale's son. "Sir William. Take him to his chamber."

The haughty William Douglas grimaced, but his father pointed at the king and said, "See to it."

William Douglas grasped James from behind, wrapping his arms around the boy, and lifted him off the ground, trapping the his arms against his chest.

The king went very still, his face pasty except for the livid red splash on his face. His eyes were wide and he spread a blue stare across men in the room, body rigid.

Patrick pressed a shaking hand to his mouth. He stared for a moment at James Douglas of Avondale as a truth dawned. The man was the Earl of Douglas's cousin. Only just married with no child, Avondale was also his heir. No wonder he had suddenly appeared in Edinburgh. With an icy wave of horror, he wondered how long they had planned this travesty.

Callendar speared Patrick with a glare. "See that the king remains in his chamber. I shall supervise that the executions are promptly carried out."

Patrick's stomach roiled, and he stared at Callendar in revulsion.

Pointing after the boy king, Callendar said, "Go."

Patrick dashed out of the room. He rushed pell-mell through the hall and up the stairs, shoving aside a servant who got in his way. By the time he caught up, William Douglas was kicking the door open to the king's bedchamber, his arms still wrapped around the boy.

Patrick seized Douglas's arm and jerked him around. "Let him go!"

Patrick let go of the arm and raised a fist, but Douglas still held the lad before him.

Douglas's eye's narrowed. He dropped James to his feet. "Very well. But you will keep him to his chamber if you ken you're wise." He bared his teeth in a sneer. "And the next time you lay a hand on me, you'll lose it."

"You laid hands on the king!" Patrick shouted, but Douglas had already turned and was swaggering away. He slammed the door behind him.

James slowly raised his head to look up at Patrick, his face stark white. The birthmark stood out like a bloodstain. His chest heaved. His expression seemed frozen with horror, but his eyes blazed. He looked as though he might go mad with the shock. Or perhaps it was rage.

Patrick dropped to one knee and whispered, “Your Grace.”

James whirled and stormed across the room. When he came up against a table he'd seemed not even to see until he bumped in it, he beat on it with clinch fists. He hammered it again and again in speechless rage.

Patrick remained where he knelt. What could he possible say to his young king?

Finally the king turned, stilled. He stared at the wall for a long moment. When he turned, his hands still gripped in fists, his face was still starkly pale, but there had come an almost scary calmness in his eyes.

In a low, steady voice he said, "When I am a man grown, I shall kill them."

Patrick gaped, trying to think of some answer.

The king caught Patrick in his blue gaze. "Oh, I shall kill them, Sir Patrick. I make a solemn oath. I dinnae ken when, but I shall kill them."

"I believe you, Your Grace," Patrick whispered. He rose, looked around the chamber, and spotted a flagon of malmsey. He very much needed a drink, though one would not be enough.

He mixed a cup of wine with some water for the king. He drank his down in a long draught.

James sipped his thoughtfully. “It was all planned.”

Patrick ran his hands through his hair, tugged at it, and groaned. “Aye, I think so.” How could Crichton and Callendar take part in such a crime? What could Avondale have offered them?

James rubbed at his face and mouth with his hand and heaved a huge sigh. There was a book on the table that he flipped open with a finger. In a tone still frighteningly calm, he said, "Are they dead yet, do you suppose? I hope..."

Patrick heard his swallow from across the room. "I hope it was fast. That they did nae suffer."

At a soft knock, Patrick opened the door and Alex slipped inside. He was almost as white-faced as James. He opened his mouth, glanced at the king, and closed it. Patrick shrugged. There was no point in trying to keep from James whatever news Alex had.

Alex shook his head. "It is done. The worst thing I have ever seen, I swear to you. Young Douglas begged that they take his brother first, so the poor lad would not have to watch him die, but they dragged him to the block first." Alex rubbed his face, looking a little sick. "It took two swings of the blade to take off his head. But thank all the saints, I think he it was fast. David was crying when they killed him, like the child that he was."

Ignoring all courtesy that he not sit in the presence of the king, Patrick sank into a chair, resting his elbows on his thighs, hands limp. "What have we come to? Murdering children, guests at the king's table?"

Dear God in heaven, how could such a thing happen?

The king whispered, "They were my cousins."

Alex poured them all another cup of wine, mixed half with water for the king. Even after the horror of the evening, the wine began to make the lad sleepy. He crawled on top of the coverlets in the large bed, yawning widely. "I shan't sleep but mayhap I'll rest for a while," he murmured as his eyes closed.

Alex sat, his head dropped into his hands. He looked up, shook his head, and went back to his morose reverie.

"I need to send this news to my father and the queen. I'll be back in a few hours. If anyone comes looking for me, I went out to wench."

"Why would anyone come looking for you?"

Patrick opened the door a crack and said in a low voice, "I

dinnae think they will, but if they do, I'm looking to find a willing lass for the night." With Alex frowning after him, Patrick peered in both directions to be sure no one was about and slipped out of the room. He softly closed the door behind him.

He had to wait until most of the castle was asleep before he slipped out of the sally port where he hoped he could bribe the sole guard. He clattered up the narrow winding stairs to the top floor and the tiny chamber he was sharing with Alex.

The box bed took up most of the room other than that occupied by a small table. A few items of their clothing and his sword hung from pegs on the wall. He poured water into the bowl on the table because he felt begrimed, as though the violence of the evening had coated his skin. Hurriedly, he stripped and washed his face and hands. By the time he was finished, his teeth were chattering because the chamber was far from warm, but the feeling of being begrimed by the events stayed with him.

He turned to the small kist of belongings he had brought from Stirling Castle and dug through it for clothes suitable for his task. He took his time donning his clothes, linen undershirt, drawers, black woolen doublet and dark brown chauses. They were made of good Scottish wool and woven on a loom whose home he could have seen from his father's castle at Longforgan if he ever had time to go there.

He rubbed his arms to warm them, wishing rooms high in castle towers were better heated but who would waste wood or peat for such frivolities? It was a room assigned to the least important guests in the castle and did not rate any luxury. He donned his cloak, dark blue but he had no other with him.

The stairway was dark and he bumped into a man coming up. "Watch it," the man grumbled, "or I'll give you a skelp you will nae forget."

"Sorry. I did nae see you," he said and forced a laugh.

The man grunted and stumped past. He made his way in the pitch dark to near the bottom of the stairs and through the short corridor. There was some light from the great hall where there was a sound of muted confusion was the servants settled for the night.

Head down he stepped into the vast room. It was largely empty now, the trestle tables all moved out of the way. One of the man-servants was putting out the torches with a cup at the end of a long pole because they were on the wall in sconces a full ten or twelve feet off the floor. Several other men were dragging in thin straw mats since most of the castle servants slept near the hearth in the great hall.

Head down, Patrick wended his way through the dying confusion, not that any servant would question him. But he preferred that if possible no one would know about his movements. He counted on their tiredness to keep them from noticing. None of them so much as glanced his way when he opened the door and slipped out into the night.

High in the tower, tiny bars of light showed that a few people had not yet retired. There was not another touch of light. The stars were hidden behind thick clouds and the moon made only a faint nimbus in them. He made his way by touch along the wall. He'd spent no time at Edinburgh Castle since their flight, but he knew it well enough that he didn't need to see. He stepped carefully, trying not to make any noise, not that he didn't have the right to be out in the night, but he didn't want to have to explain why. And God only knew what orders Crichton might have given.

Patrick stopped and held his breath as he listened. The castle might have been abandoned it was so silent with not a sound of breathing or a scrape of boot leather. No one was about.

There were only two ways out of Edinburgh Castle, the

main gate to the east and a sally gate in the north wall. Both opened into the outer bailey. The gate to the inner bailey would already be closed and barred, completely shut off from the outer bailey. There was no way through, so he'd have to go over.

Nearby there were stairs that went up onto the bailey wall walk for defense if the outer bailey were taken. He continued to feel his way until he bumped into the first step and stumbled. Keeping one shoulder against the wall he crept up the stairs stepping as quietly as he could. He had never seen men-at-arms patrolling this wall, hardly needed with the strong outer wall, but he couldn't be sure if that had changed.

At the top of the steps, he crouched and eased his head had above the level of the wall walk. He looked left and right. He waited for the sound of the footstep or a sign of movement. At last, he crawled onto the walkway, keeping down to be sure no sign of his silhouette showed above the crenellations. His hand landed in an icy puddle that was nasty with slime. He grimaced and wiped it on his cloak. That convinced him to rise enough to crouch walk to peer between two of the merlons. As far as he knew no men-at-arms walked a patrol in the inner bailey except on the far parapet walks, and there was no sign of any movement below. It was a good drop, at least fifteen feet, so he slid feet over, and grasped the edge until he was hanging by his fingertips. He let go.

He landed hard, with bent knees. Silently cursing, heart pounding, he waited. It had made a thump when he landed. Next to the wall, the dark was complete, so he stayed motionless, waiting for a cry of waring. In the distance, there were footfalls, steady and even: a guard walking his post. A door creaked as it opened and a square of light was thrown from a guardroom. It slammed shut and the night was dark again.

Patrick rubbed his knees. The landing had been hard, but no harm done. Slowly, carefully, he stood. Was the risk greater for walking openly that someone might see him or creeping and giving away that he was spying? He waited. There was no reason the men-at-arms would watch in bailey. The danger would be outside the walls from Douglas men seeking their master. So as quietly as he could, but trying to look as though he were merely strolling, he walked next to the wall across the bailey and to the sally gate.

The guard called out, "Who goes there?"

"Wheesht," Patrick whispered. "It's Sir Patrick Gray."

"What the devil are you doing creeping about out here?" the guard demanded.

"There's a lass in a tavern I visit when we're in Edinburgh." He tried to sound embarrassed. "And they have good ale there."

"The gates are closed."

"Of course they are. But if you open it just enough for me to slip out no one will ever be the wise." He nudged the man with his elbow and put a smile in his voice. "And I have more coins in my purse than I should carry about at night."

The man grunted. "Well, you're not the first fool to go wandering about Edinburgh at night. But Lord Crichton would have me flogged—"

Patrick let some coins clink as he pulled a couple out of his purse. "It was a bad day," he said softly. "I just want to have a soft armful and a drink to take the bad taste away."

The man blew out a noisy breath and put out his hand for the coins. "Aye, very well. That it was a bad day, but I never seen you. And if his lordship has your hide, 'tis no business of mine."

They both looked around to be sure no one was in sight. The guard grunted as he hefted the beam that barred the heavy gate. Patrick pushed the gate open barely enough to slip out, and it shut behind him with two thuds, the closing of the door and the dropping of the bar.

19

Patrick's shuffled softly on the stony path around the castle wall in the dark and then thudded down the cobbles of the Via Regis. The houses along the broad street, which in daytime jutted high on both sides, loomed like the sides of a deep crevasse.

He hurried down the incline of the street, head down and wary. Once he loosened his sword in its scabbard, for a man alone, even armed, would be a tempting target for thieves. But the day's events circled and skittered in his mind like frightened mice eager to escape. He was convinced that Avondale was behind the executions, for it was he who would profit, he and his heir. But why had Callendar and Crichton agreed to the terrible act? What could he have promised them? The Douglas had supported Crichton as chancellor, so why would he turn against the earl? Of course, that had been the lad's father, but the young Douglas had seemed to show no enmity to his father's old ally. He knew of greed, but double murder at the king's own table to steal an earldom? It made no sense.

He had to send word to his father and hope older heads

would know what it all meant. He had just turned onto Duddingston Low Road toward the Sheep Heid Inn when he heard a scrape of movement behind him. He slowed and took another few steps and there it was again, the faint scrape of a shoe in the dirt.

At the next ally between two tall houses, he slipped around the corner and dropped into a low crouch. He peeked back around the corner. A shadow crept toward him keeping close to the edge of the street. It was a thin, reedy figure that moved silently except for a scape of his shoe leather, not a man in armor. Patrick silently drew his dirk and waited. The shadowy figure peered around the corner. Patrick grabbed him.

Slippery as a weasel, the thin man squirmed free before Patrick could tighten his hold. He reached behind his back and came out with a dagger. He thrust at Patrick's throat.

Patrick shuffled back a step. He traded his dirk to his left hand and drew his sword, keeping his narrow gaze on his opponent's face. The man facing him was scrawny and young. Even a scrawny man with a dagger is dangerous though and Patrick couldn't be sure he didn't have an ally somewhere nearby.

"What do you want?" Patrick asked.

"Nuffin'." The thief backed up a step, as though to give himself space. He lowered his dagger to his hip as he crouched. He obviously knew his business and this wasn't the first man he'd attacked.

"Good because that is what you are getting." Patrick lifted his sword a little higher so it was near the thief's throat. Truthfully, he'd rather not kill the poor gutter rat, but he would if he had to. "If I see you near me again, next time you'll not live to steal again." Patrick eased around the man, who wheeled to keep him in sight.

Patrick backed up a couple of steps before he sheathed

his sword. He pointed his dirk in the thief's direction and said, "Best you nae forget it." And then he turned on his heel and strode off the way he had been going. He glanced behind him once, to see a silhouette in the distance, but he blew out a breath. The thief seemed to have given up.

This late, the gate to the yard of the Sheep Heid Inn was barred, of course. Patrick jumped and grabbed the top, pulled himself up and threw a leg over. He dropped into the yard hard enough that the yard dog, chained near the door, awoke and barked. There was shuffling inside as though someone had awakened and a glow of a candle gleamed through the shutters. Patrick scrambled for the stable as the dog's bark lowered to a growl.

When he closed the door, someone in the back mumbled, "What's to-do?"

Patrick let out a breath of relief. He'd feared that the friar who had accompanied him might have gone off, but Patrick was, finally, in luck. "Wheesht. It's Sir Patrick Gray." He tiptoed to the back stall where a begging friar was sometimes allowed a little space in the hay by the inn's owner as alms.

A horse nickered. Another stuck it head out to look at him. Patrick felt his way back in the deep gloom. Brother Symond was asleep in the last stall. Patrick dropped to his knees in the narrow doorway. It was a small stall, used for storing hay and tack. In the back bales were piled up to the ceiling. In one corner, Brother Symon lay curled on a bed of hay lay stretched out beneath a horse blanket. Like the hay, it belonged to the inn because Symon said that owning a blanket would violate his oath of poverty. Tack hung from pegs on the wall as did Brother Symond's brown habit with its short hood.

There was a rustling in the pile of hay before Brother Symon's sat up. He furiously rubbed his tonsured head. "If you're out carousing, you've come to the wrong place," he complained.

Patrick leaned back against the wall and slowly slid down until he was sitting, knees bent. He folded his arms across them and rested his forehead on them. His next breath was nearer a sob than he cared to admit. "I wish I were carousing." He voice croaked so he cleared his throat. "I need you to take a message to my lord father. There was..." He swallowed. Be damned if he would weep like a bairn. "Something happened at the castle."

"What has happened? There were many shouts and a crowd at Carlton Hill, but I thought it best to stay clear."

Patrick leaned his head back against the rough boards of the wall. "It's bad. They..." He swallowed again. "They killed the Earl of Douglas today and his young brother. The called it a trial but it was judicial murder. Dragged them from the king's own table..."

Symon crossed himself, muttering, "*Requiēscat in pāce.*" But then his curiosity seemed to get the better of him. He cocked his head. "How did it happen? Who did it? Crichton?"

"The Earl of Avondale and Callendar. I think they were mainly behind it but Crichton had a hand in it too."

"Avondale?" Brother Symon tugged on his short beard. "The fat one, aye?"

"He is Douglas's heir. They destroyed the last of that line."

Patrick slammed his head back against the boards. "And there was nae a Satan be-damned thing I could do to stop them."

The monk was slowly shaking his head. "The earl would have had guest rights. At the king's own table."

"Aye."

The friar nodded thoughtfully. "Aye, since Bishop

Kennedy is nae within reach, it is best we get word of this to your father and to the queen."

"I dinnae ken if Avondale just wants the riches and title or if he..." He waved a hand vaguely. "...if he plans something more. But they need to ken so they will nae be taken by surprise and mayhap they can send word to Bishop Kennedy. We need him here, nae in Florence arguing with fat clerics."

"Avondale is an old man though. He cannot be that long for the world. Mayhap he wants the title for his own heir."

"He is old, right enough. He must be seventy years if he is a day and fat as a sow. But neither keep him from scheming" Patrick squinted at Brother Symon but he couldn't make out his face in the dark. "Would a man murder like that for riches for a son?"

"There are men who will do any evil you can imagine. What about his son? What kind of man is he? Do you think he might have pressed his father to do this?"

"He's young, but proud and..." Patrick shook his head. "It is hard to describe. Aye, he wants power. He has a sneer that sets badly with me. He kent it was going to happen before it did. That I can tell you. He might have pressed his father, although I dinnae ken how much pressing it would have taken."

"Och, 'tis not for the likes of us to unravel. So where is your father now? With the queen mother at Dunbar?"

"Aye. The last word I had that's where he was and if he has left the queen must know and send word to him."

Brother Symon threw back his blanket. "They'll nae open the doors for you at the inn this late, so you'll do penance for your sins sleeping on the floor."

"I have a thick cloak, and if I sleep it will truly be a miracle. Any road, I dinnae want to noise about what I have been doing, so I'll just sit here until daylight."

"Aye, I shall be off. I can talk my way past the guards at

the gate. Do you have siller to buy me some bread for the journey? If I dinnae have to worrit on begging for alms on the way, it will speed me."

"Certes. Take bread and cheese. A canteen of ale as well. I thank you for this, Brother." He emptied his scrip into the friar's hand, and then sighed and closed his eyes. "I just wish..." But there had been nothing he could have done. His stomach churned as though he had taken a hard blow. That there was nothing he could have done made me feel not even a whit better that he had stood by while those boys were murdered.

He stared into the star-strewn night sky long after the monk had trudged out of sight. A frigid wind whipped though the stable as words seemed to echo in the night air:

When I am a man grown, I shall kill them.

Please watch for Book 4 of the Stewart Chronicle out in 2018.

GLOSSARY

- Aught — Anything at all.
- Aye — Yes.
- Bailey — An enclosed courtyard within the walls of a castle.
- Bairn — Child.
- Barbican — A tower or other fortification on the approach to a castle or town, Especially one at a gate or drawbridge.
- Battlement — A parapet in which rectangular gaps occur at intervals to allow for firing arrows.
- Bedecked — To adorn or ornament in a showy fashion.
- Brae — Hill or slope.
- Barmy — Daft.
- Bonnie — Handsome or attractive.
- Braw — Fine or excellent.
- Burgher — A citizen of a borough or town, especially one belonging to middle class.
- Burn — A name for watercourses from large streams to small rivers.

- Cannae — Cannot.
- Chancel — The space around the altar at the liturgical east end.
- Courser — A swift, strong horse, often used as a warhorse.
- Crenel — An open space or notch between two merlons in the battlement of a castle or city wall.
- Curtain wall — The defensive outer wall of a medieval castle.
- Dagged — A series of decorative scallops along the edge of a garment such as a hanging sleeve.
- Dirk — A long, straight-bladed dagger.
- Dower — The part or interest of a deceased man's real estate allotted by law to his widow for her lifetime, often applied to property brought to the marriage by the bride.
- Draught — Drafty or a long drink
- Duniwassal — A minor Highland nobleman.
- Faggot — A bundle of sticks or twigs, esp. when bound together and used as fuel.
- Fash — Worry.
- Forbye — Besides.
- Ford — A shallow crossing in a body of water, such as a river.
- Gentleman of the Bedchamber — An office that involved waiting upon the king in private, helping him to dress, guarding his bedchamber, and providing companionship.
- Gey — Very.
- Groat — An English silver coin worth four pence.
- Hurlyhacket - a children's game of sliding down a hill often in a chain holding onto one another.
- Haugh — A low-lying meadow in a river valley.

- Hen — An affectionate term of address used to women and girls.
- Hied — To go quickly; hasten.
- Hodden-gray — Coarse woolen cloth made from a mix of white and dark fleece.
- Holy Rood — The Holy Cross
- Jesu — Vocative form of Jesus.
- Ken — To know (a person or thing). Kent is the past tense.
- Kirk — A church.
- Loch — Lake.
- Louring, Lowering.
- Malmsey — A sweet fortified Madeira wine
- Marischal — The hereditary custodian of the Royal Regalia of Scotland and protector of the king's person.
- Merk — Scottish coin worth 160 pence.
- Merlon — A solid portion between two crenels in a battlement or crenellated wall.
- Midges — A gnat-like fly found worldwide and frequently occurring in swarms near ponds and lakes, prevalent across Scotland
- Nae — No, Not.
- Outwith — Outside, beyond.
- Parapet — A defensive wall, usually with a walk, above which the wall is chest to head high.
- Privily — Privately or secretly.
- Quintain — Object mounted on a post, used as a target in tilting exercises
- Saltire — An ordinary in the shape of a Saint Andrew's cross, when capitalized: the flag of Scotland. (a white saltire on a blue field)
- Samite — A heavy silk fabric, often interwoven with gold or silver.

- Sassenach — An Englishman or sometimes a Scottish lowlander, derived from the Scots Gaelic Sasunnach meaning, originally, "Saxon."
- Siller — Silver.
- Sleekit, —Unctuous, deceitful, crafty.
- Tail — A noble's following of men-at-arms.
- Trencher — A plate or platter for food, sometimes formed by a slice of bread.
- Trestle table — A table made up of two or three trestle supports over which a tabletop is placed.
- Well-found — Well equipped, having everything needed or desirable.
- Westering — To move westward.
- Whilst — While.
- Wheesht — To be silent, often used as an interjection to urge silence.
- Worrit — Worry
- Wroth — Angry.
- Vennel — Small side street or alley.

HISTORICAL NOTES

Exact details of the early reign of Scotland's King James II are surprisingly difficult to come by. A number of early reigns are in fact easier to research. I used as many original sources as possible, none of which are easily accessible to most readers. One of the few readily available books on his remarkable years as King of Scots is *James II* by Christine McGladdery. While *The Life and Times of James Kennedy, Bishop of St. Andrews* by Annie I. Dunlop overstates the role of Kennedy at times, it also provides an interesting view into a tumultuous and violent period of Scottish history.

ALSO BY J. R. TOMLIN

A King Ensnared - Stewart Chronicle Book 1

A King Uncaged - The Stewart Chronicle Book 2

Freedom's Sword - Prequel to The Black Douglas Trilogy

A Kingdom's Cost - The Black Douglas Trilogy Book 1

Countenance of War - The Black Douglas Trilogy Book 2

Not for Glory - The Black Douglas Trilogy Book 3

The Templar's Cross: A Medieval Mystery (The Sir Law Kintour Series Book 1)

The Winter Kill: A Medieval Mystery (The Sir Law Kintour Series Book 2)

The Intelligencer: A Medieval Mystery (The Sir Law Kintour Mysteries Book 3)

ABOUT THE AUTHOR

J. R. Tomlin is the author of ten historical novels. All are set in medieval Scotland with portions taking place in Engalnd or France.

She has close ties with Scotland since her father was a native Scot, and she spent substantial time in Edinburgh whilst growing up. Her love of that nation is traced from the stories of the Bruce and the Good Sir James her grandmother read to her when she was small, to hillwalking through the Cairngorms where the granite hills have a gorgeous red glow under the setting sun. Later, her writing was influenced by the work of authors such as Alexander Dumas, Victor Hugo, and of course, J.R.R. Tolkien.

When JR isn't writing, she enjoys spending time hiking, playing with her Westie, and killing monsters in computer games. In addition to spending time in Scotland, she has traveled in the US, Europe and the Pacific Rim. She now lives in Oregon.

Made in the USA
Lexington, KY
01 November 2017